TRAIL OF THE FEARLESS GUN

Chance Darringer is coming back to Tombstone, hoping to marry the woman of his dreams. But when he arrives to pop the question, Polly is lying dead on her sewing-room floor, brutally beaten. Chance has a clue about who may have done the killing, and he decides to trail Oscar Rawlins and his gang. At least one woman and countless men have fallen prey to Oscar's evil ways, and as long as Chance Darringer is alive, there won't be another!

Books by Lee Martin
in the Linford Western Library:

DEAD MAN'S WALK
TRAIL OF THE HUNTER
TRAIL OF THE CIRCLE STAR
TRAIL OF THE FAST GUN
TRAIL OF THE LONG RIDERS
TRAIL OF THE RESTLESS GUN

LEE MARTIN

TRAIL OF THE FEARLESS GUN

Complete and Unabridged

LINFORD
Leicester

First published in the
United States of America

First Linford Edition
published 2000

British Library CIP Data

Martin, Lee, *1943 –*
    Trail of the fearless gun.—Large print ed.—
Linford western library
1. Western stories
2. Large type books
I. Title
813.5'4 [F]

ISBN 0–7089–5745–5

Published by
F. A. Thorpe (Publishing)
Anstey, Leicestershire

Set by Words & Graphics Ltd.
Anstey, Leicestershire
Printed and bound in Great Britain by
T. J. International Ltd., Padstow, Cornwall

This book is printed on acid-free paper

To my godson Jack Kidrick Martin, a wild and woolly cowboy, of whom I am very proud, and to his lovely wife, Cindy, and sons, Alec and J.J.

1

All the way from Texas, Chance Darringer told himself that Polly would say yes. Now, as he rode into Tombstone, where tents and shacks lined the dusty street, his bravado was falling apart. Last fall, he had been here with his twin brother and his cousins, delivering horses to Fort Lowell. He had lost his senses over Polly and had promised he would return in the spring of 1879.

Now, he was crumbling. Men would be camped on her doorstep. Polly was as pretty as a Texas sunrise, with her golden hair, brown eyes, pert nose, quick laugh, and sense of humor. Being around her had turned him into jelly.

He needed a bath and change of clothes. His dark-brown hair was thick with trail dust, which had reddened his brown eyes. His hard, square face, with a slight hook to his nose, was burned by the sun. Six feet tall, he wore twin Colts because he was as good with one hand as the other. But as brave as he was around men, he was an idiot around women.

He reined his buckskin stallion to a halt in front of the livery. After taking care of his mount, he walked to the barber shop for a bath in an iron tub in the back room.

Soaking in the water, he remembered his last sight of Polly. She had called to him from the porch of her mother's home.

'Please come back, Chance Darringer.'

He clung to that memory, determined to build up his courage. After changing into fresh new Levi's and a blue double-breasted shirt, he had a shave. His hair was trimmed to his collar.

Anxiety gripped him again. He was a cowboy whose only possessions were his stallion and some unknown, future share in his father's Texas ranch empire. He had some education, but nothing fancy. He could sing a little. He even knew how to dance. But he was a cow-hand, and sometimes a gunfighter. Why hadn't he tried to get her answer by mail?

At noon, gathering his courage, he walked to the big house at the end of town and bravely pounded on the door. There was no answer. Now he was really shaking in his boots. Frantic, he turned back up the street, wondering where Polly and her mother were. No neighbors seemed to be about.

He sat on a bench in the shade near the saloon, whistling 'Red River Valley,' trying to be nonchalant even as sweat trickled down his collar. He laughed at himself.

It was then that he noticed the big, black, wolflike dog. It had appeared behind him as he rode into town, and had trailed him to the livery, then disappeared. Now it was back, watching him from about six feet away, its growl barely audible.

'You got a name, pardner?'

The dog bared its teeth. Its yellow eyes gleamed.

Deciding to ignore the creature, Chance stood up and began to wander the town, sight-seeing a little. The dog trotted behind him. Chance had something to eat at the saloon. He tossed some leftover meat to the animal. It snarled before it ate.

Soon it was four o'clock. With his heart going crazy in his chest, he walked again toward the big house at the south end of town. The dog followed him at a distance. Polly's mother had been friendly enough, but maybe she only had been polite. Maybe she wanted Polly to marry some wealthy man.

There was a buggy with a lone horse in front of the house. Someone was home at last. He reached under his Stetson to slick down his hair. Climbing the steps, he felt sweat on his back. Maybe she was already married or betrothed.

He started to knock just as the door opened. A stocky man in a leather coat and narrow-brimmed hat was standing there, his face grim. There was a scar on his left cheek.

'Don't come in here, son.' He sounded like the voice of doom.

Chance felt sudden knots in his stomach. He shoved the man aside and charged into the parlor. Polly's gray-haired mother was sitting on the couch holding a pair of sewing scissors. She looked crazed. Chance was suddenly as cold as ice.

'Where's Polly?'

The man shrugged. 'In that sewing room, but don't — '

It was too late. Chance could see through the open archway to where knitting and fabrics were scattered on the floor. A chair was overturned.

His heart erratic, he hurried into the room and saw a blanket covering a woman's figure. All he could see was her blond hair. He knelt to lift the blanket and was overwhelmed with nausea. She had been beaten to death. Blood was all over. He dropped the blanket, rearing back on his heels, crazed and disoriented.

He couldn't breathe. Then he saw something in the thickness of the rug, under the overturned chair. He picked it up. It was a gold money clip holding a single greenback. A crooked 'Rocking R' symbol with a half moon was etched on the side. He shoved it in his coat pocket.

As he regained his balance, fury welled up in him. He spun on his heel and went back to the parlor. He saw the stranger seated with Polly's mother, his arm around her.

'My name's Beale,' the man said. 'Her mother's been visitin' my sick wife at our ranch for a few days. We just got back a couple of hours ago. I dropped her mother off outside and went over to the store. Then I came back for supper. Her mother had found Polly, but I can't get nothin' out of her. Doc was here and said the girl's been dead a long time, since last night.'

Beale tried to get the woman to

speak to him. Instead, Polly's mother just stayed in a trance. She had escaped reality in the only way she could bear her pain.

Chance stumbled outside into the cool evening. Beale followed. It was a while before Chance could draw a breath. He felt his face burning, his mouth dry. When he had knocked on the door at noon, Polly had been lying there in her own blood. Knots were still in his throat when he managed to speak.

'You got any law around here?'

'No, but we got a meetin' planned to set up the town of Tombstone. That's our first step. But there's miner's law. Maybe we can get the miner's court to do somethin'.'

'I ain't waitin'. You recognize this brand?' He showed the money clip to Beale, who nodded.

'That's the Rawlins outfit. Got a ranch near Antler, up north, on the other side of the White Mountains. They was here when I picked up

7

Polly's mother. They'd brung some cattle down to sell at one of the silver mines. I was talkin' to a fellow in the outfit, named Grimey. Big man. He said they'd mainly come to pick up some woman who was goin' to marry Rawlins's son.'

'They still here?'

'No. When I was at the saloon a while ago, the barkeep said they left early this mornin'. He was sorry, as they had been big spenders. You see 'em on the trail?'

'No, I took a short cut. How will I find them?'

With his boot, the man drew a map in the dirt of the street. Chance watched and listened, a cold fist in his stomach. He pocketed the money clip.

'I'm gonna track them if I have to go all the way to Antler.'

'That's a mean outfit, son. About six or seven of 'em. You be careful.'

Chance headed for the livery, the dog following some ten feet behind. He fought back his tears as he collected his stallion and went to the store for more provisions. It would be dark in a few hours, but he couldn't wait. Soon, he was on the trail to the northwest. All he could think of was Polly's laughter. Her pretty brown eyes. The way she had won his heart.

'You're such a ninny,' she had laughed.

He was forced to camp because his horse was still weary after the journey from Texas. The dog still snarled at him, but he fed it from a distance.

'Part wolf, ain't you?'

The dog bared its teeth, but lay only a few feet away.

Chance wept a few tears that night, but the rest stayed buried in his heart. He found no relief. He was hurt too deep. Before dawn, he continued on his way northwest, certain he knew the direction to the river pass to Antler. The man's map had been pretty straight-forward.

A day later, he reached the old stage

road that cut west to east. The wide-open land was covered with green along the creek beds. Palo verde bloomed yellow and bright. Flowers of white and red opened on cacti. And the black dog still trotted along behind him.

The land changed with every drifting cloud. Often it was crimson and rich with wild blooms. Sometimes it looked gray and wasted, the distant rock formations forbidding. The path often shifted around tall saguaro and thick prickly pear.

Chance knew that to the east lay Apache Pass, Fort Bowie, and Texas. But he was heading north to the White Mountains. He soon discovered the trail of eight saddle horses and a pack mule. He figured it was the Rawlins outfit.

Days later, in the hot afternoon, he could read signs that the outfit was only a few hours ahead. He was gaining on them, thanks to his big buckskin. And his own fury had settled into a hard knot in his middle. A flood of tears was still buried in his heart, but he couldn't rest until the killer hanged. Then he would sit down and cry.

Chance reined up to look at the tracks. The outfit had turned directly north on a beaten path across rolling prairie — right over the tracks of Apache boots. A woman's yellow scarf with white dots lay in the dust.

It was then he heard the distant gunfire to the north.

Without hesitating, he leaned from his saddle and scooped up the silk scarf, tucking it in his belt. Then he set his horse to a gallop and bent low in the saddle. Riding full speed across the desert in the late-afternoon sun, he could think only of the Apache.

Maybe the killer was with the Rawlins outfit, but the others deserved to live. And there was a woman with them. He couldn't bear to see another woman covered with blood.

The camp ahead was nestled in a circle of rocks and rolling high ground. Blue sage crowded the area. The horses and the lone mule were half unsaddled and hobbled some distance from the fighting.

Charging toward the besieged camp, Chance was first into the circle. Eight Apache in the brush and rocks were in hand-to-hand struggle with the cowhands.

The warriors were bare chested, their bodies powerful and gleaming. Their faces were hard and square with high, wide cheekbones and powerful jaws. White scarves bound their heads. One Apache was enough to terrorize a town.

Then Chance saw a strange and terrible sight near the campfire.

A big Apache had a screaming little girl of maybe ten in his grasp, one hand gripping her yellow curls. A young woman of maybe twenty was on his back, her arms around his neck in a viselike grip. She had his left ear in her teeth. Roaring mad, he threw the child to the hard ground. The girl rolled over and then crawled away frantically to hide in a ditch.

The Apache fought to shake the woman from his back. Her legs jerked free of him and flew in the air. His powerful fingers tore at her arms. When he shook her loose, she was thrown in a heap to the ground. With knife in hand, the furious warrior was about to turn on her. Chance shot him twice in the chest.

But the Apache was still alive, charging forward and reaching for the buckskin's bridle. Chance shot him again. The warrior died on his feet, eyes still wild with hate as he crumpled to the ground.

A huge, bearded man with massive shoulders was kneeling behind rocks some ten feet from the campfire. His left arm was cut open. A bleeding, white-bearded man was crawling in the rocks. Another cowhand, arrows in his body, lay face-down in the nearby wash by a shallow water hole. Two more were in the rocks fighting with the warriors.

A stocky, red-bearded man was on

top of a dead Apache, still beating him. It was a horrid sight, the crazed man pounding a lifeless warrior. His gray eyes were wild, his cruel mouth twisted.

Suddenly, Chance was pulled from his horse by a powerful Apache. They rolled in the red dust, struggling for control of the warrior's knife. Sweat covered Chance's face. The Apache was too strong. Chance tricked him with a left-handed blow and a feint of his right fist, which grabbed the knife. He forced the blade down into the warrior's middle. When it was over, Chance rolled free, panting for breath.

He turned, rising on one knee. The firing had stopped. A terrible silence reigned. The Apache were all dead. The giant man with the cut arm was making a wide circle, rifle in hand, looking for signs of life. Then he returned, beard twitching.

'That's all there was.'

Chance stood up. The little girl came out of the ditch. The young woman, tears on her blood-spotted cheeks, sat up and stared at Chance, her dark-blue eyes round and fearful. There was a slight turn up at the end of her small nose. She bowed her head with her face in her hands, shaking all over. Golden-brown hair fell in waves about her.

The red-bearded man, his piercing gray eyes still crazed, staggered around the death scene. He was stocky with powerful arms. There was blood on his hands. His cruel mouth was twisted in fury, and hate raged in his face.

'That's our boss, Oscar Rawlins,' the giant said. 'My name's Grimey. And that's Miss Susanna Ward. The little girl is Becky, her sister.'

Chance looked at the red-bearded man. Oscar Rawlins. He'd be the one to carry a money clip with his brand. He acted weird enough to have killed any woman who resisted his advances. Chance felt his stomach tying in knots.

But the giant, Grimey, looked more like a friendly bear who probably wouldn't hurt a horsefly. Still, one of these men could have murdered Polly. And he was with them.

Grimey went over to the white-bearded man and found him conscious but still stunned, and helped him rise. The old cowhand, who was addressed as Tolliver, wiped the blood from his face. He looked like an old-timer who'd been riding trail all his life, seasoned and weathered, fearless and determined to survive. Chance respected men like him.

The other three cowhands were as grizzled. One named Hutch was dead. Another, called Borcher, was an ugly man with a big nose and black mustache. He appeared mean as sin. He was the kind of man who would as soon stab you as look at you. That kind of man could kill a woman without hesitation.

The third man was named Lynch. He had big shoulders and skinny hands. His left eye was almost closed from some old injury. He looked mean as a wild pig. There was no doubt that

Lynch hated the world and could kill without hesitation. After a hard look at Chance, he turned and walked over to Oscar.

Chance took their measure. Now that the fight with the Apache was over, he felt the thirst for vengeance like hot fire in his chest again. One of these men could be his prey. He was certain of it. His pain would never ease until Polly's killer was punished, one way or another.

Grimey helped Tolliver to the fireside, then knelt as he spoke to Chance. 'We was busy hobblin' the horses over yonder when they hit us. One of them grabbed Becky. Did you see Susanna?'

Becky nodded, blue eyes wide. 'She saved me.'

'It happened fast,' Grimey said. 'And there was no sign of 'em before. We could see for miles. There were no tracks around the water hole. Nothin'.'

'They were on foot,' Chance said. 'An Apache can just about outrun a horse. But seems likely they knew you were comin' and buried themselves in the sand and just waited.'

'We ain't got your name,' Oscar Rawlins snapped.

'Darringer. Chance Darringer.'

'Well, now,' Oscar said. 'One of the wild ones, eh?'

Susanna looked up slowly, wiping the blood from her face with the back of her hand. The Apache's head had likely hit her nose and mouth. She looked all right, but she was still shaking. Becky went over to kneel and hug her sister. With a canteen and a handkerchief, she washed Susanna's face. The men tended their own wounds.

'Mighty glad you came our way,' Grimey said.

Chance nodded and told them he was headed for Montana. He had only one clue to Polly's killer. It was better he smell the man out first. He wanted to be right. And he didn't want to be murdered in his sleep. He had to move slowly, something that had never come naturally.

The big dog came trotting up, its tongue hanging. It dropped down near them, exhausted. Tolliver sat with his head down, still shaken. His hands were trembling.

Oscar Rawlins had calmed down, but he obviously didn't like having a Darringer in the camp. Yet he swallowed his displeasure because he had lost a man. And he was a little nervous now that the attack was over. In fact, his hands were shaking as he tried to roll a cigarette.

The men dragged the dead Indians away from camp. Chance insisted on covering them with rocks and dirt to protect them from vultures. When the others turned back toward camp, Chance paused, hat over his heart, feeling sad for the brave warriors whose land they had invaded.

He whispered softly, 'They fought a good fight, Lord. Give 'em peace, and a lot of room to hunt.'

He turned back to camp. The dead cowhand was given a separate burial.

Susanna and Becky cried, Tolliver was sad, but Lynch and Borcher weren't even interested. Out of duty, Oscar stood nearby. Hat in hand, Grimey said words over the grave.

'Hutch wasn't much with a gun. And he wasn't much for talkin'. But he had a good heart. And he knew more about cattle than any man I ever knew. And, Lord, we figure maybe You got a job for him up there. You gotta keep him busy, Lord, because he sure likes to play cards.'

Chance was touched by the big man's words. He had been right about him. If the killer was here, it wasn't Grimey.

They ate their supper in the moonlight. Susanna kept looking at Chance's belt. He suddenly realized he still had the scarf. His face turned warm. He had carried her banner into battle. Embarrassed, he pulled it free of his belt and handed it to her awkwardly.

'Is this why you came?' she asked.

Chance shrugged. 'Darringers never avoid a fight, ma'am. We got no sense.'

She managed a lovely smile as she put her arm around Becky. 'You knew we were in danger?'

Oscar Rawlins glared at the exchange. 'We'd have fought 'em off. Most of 'em were dead when you got here.'

Chance leaned forward to push sand over the flickering fire. Soon the smoke was gone. They downed the rest of the hot coffee. Susanna and Becky wrapped themselves in their blankets against the cold, but they were shivering. Even though she had the extra blankets from the dead man, Becky's face was white.

As Chance draped one of his own blankets over Susanna's shoulder where she sat, her blue eyes glistened with tears of gratitude. Her golden-brown hair was unkempt and matted about her throat. She was bruised, shattered, and tired. But she smiled up at him.

He turned and saw Oscar glaring at him. Every time Chance looked at him, he wanted to slam his fist on that cruel mouth. If Oscar would beat a dead man, there was no telling how deep the evil went.

As Susanna and Becky slept, huddled together, the big dog moved over and lay across their feet. Its yellow eyes were fixed on Chance.

Still dazed, Tolliver turned into his blankets to sleep off his pain. Oscar rolled into his bedding and was soon snoring softly. Lynch, a real hater of people, took his blankets and went off by the horses. Borcher took first watch.

Chance and Grimey sat around what had been the campfire. They kept their voices low.

Grimey wiped his brow. 'Them's Silas Rawlins's nieces. They ain't blood kin, but if anything had happened to 'em, he'd have skinned me alive. If Oscar hadn't shot me first, that is. I'm the only one who knows this trail.'

'Not a good place for women.'

'Miss Susanna's gonna marry Oscar, who's Silas's only son. It was set up when she was sixteen. They was only

22

related by marriage on her mother's side. Her folks are dead. She and Becky got no other kin. But Susanna had never met Oscar till we picked 'em up at a mine near Tombstone.'

The men continued to talk quietly as Grimey explained that their route would soon be safe. San Carlos and the Apache reservation were to the west. They would be turning northeast from the water hole. Chance repeated that he was heading for Montana. It was a natural direction to explain why he was here.

'I'll see you through to Antler.'

'Mighty obliged.'

Chance spoke of Texas. Grimey had no folks, but he had traveled far and wide. They talked of the electric lights back East. And how a bank in New York was robbed of over three million dollars. They spoke of the yellow fever raging through New Orleans.

Chance kept glancing at Susanna's lovely face as she lay sleeping. The starlight glistened on her hair. He thought of Polly, his heart aching. The dog snuggled close against Susanna's knee while keeping its gaze on Chance. Its tail hadn't wagged once.

Chance sat in silence, remembering the way Oscar had beat the already dead Apache. The man became crazed in a fight. He was not only a killer, he was a madman. He could be the one, but so could Lynch, with his one good eye and evil sneer — or Borcher with his hateful look.

Taking a deep breath, Chance took a risk and pulled out the money clip. His hand was sweaty. A lot was riding on this. He showed it to Grimey, the gold glittering in the moonlight.

'You ever seen this before?'

'Oh, sure. Last roundup, Silas Rawlins gave us all one as a bonus for not losin' hardly any cattle on the drive. We was pleased as punch. A few of them clips been won and lost in poker games. I still got mine. I think ole Borcher has a couple. So does Lynch. Oscar carries several. He gives 'em to women for favors. You know, like payment.'

Chance felt sweat on his back. Favors? Had Oscar or Lynch or Borcher offered this piece of precious metal to Polly? And for what? Sick to his stomach, he stared at the clip as it lay in his rough hand.

'Know whose this is?'

'No idea. You find it somewhere?'

'Yeah, somewhere.'

Grimey got up and headed for his blankets.

Disappointed, Chance shoved the shiny clip back in his pocket. He felt like punching the ground. He would have to find another way to expose the killer. Even though anyone in Tombstone could have gotten his hands on the clip, Chance was certain the killer was here. He could feel the scent of the kill.

Everyone else was soon asleep, except Borcher on guard. Chance sat by himself and checked his guns, his thoughts churning over the money clip. He cleaned the chambers and barrel. The other men snored softly around him. He reloaded and holstered his weapons.

His grief was so bottled up, he felt he might explode. He had loved Polly with all his heart. He had prayed she would marry him. Now she was gone, but her sweet laughter would haunt him forever.

Chance started to reach for his blankets when he saw Susanna sit up. The dog rolled aside and curled up with Becky.

Susanna slid across the ground, dragging her blankets with her. 'Every time I close my eyes, I see the Apache.'

'You were pretty brave.'

She flushed. 'I went wild when he grabbed Becky.'

He sat cross-legged and watched her bring her blankets around her chin. She was soft, pink, lovely. The moonlight caressed her hair and made her large eyes luminous. Every time he looked at her, he thought of Polly.

'Those Apache must hate us,' she said quietly.

'You're right about that.'

She glanced back toward Becky. 'Is that your dog?'

'I ain't sure. He's been followin' me, but he won't let me touch him. Seems like he took to you, all right.'

'Is he afraid of you?'

'I don't figure he's afraid of anything.'

She smiled a pretty smile. Bruised and battered, she was still lovely to look at. It was a mighty shame she was going to marry Oscar.

Some of the men moved in their blankets. She lowered her voice to a whisper. 'I'm a little afraid of the Rawlinses.'

'Why is that?'

'My mother died in California when Becky was born. My father was killed in the mines near Tombstone last fall. He left nothing. I had no way to take care of Becky. And it was my mother's dying wish that I marry Oscar, as she was related to them by marriage. So we wrote to them. But I heard the men say bad things about my Uncle Silas.'

'What folks say ain't always true.'

'Folks say the Darringers are gun-fighters.'

He shrugged. 'Well, some of my kin are. But me and my brother Cole, and my cousins, we're just ranch hands.'

She smiled at his two sidearms. 'Are you?'

Chance was amused by her twinkling eyes. 'You got a point, I reckon.'

She tried to stand, caught her foot in her blanket, and lost her balance. As she started to fall, Chance sprang to one knee and reached for her.

She tumbled back into his arms, settling on his knee and falling against his chest. Her face was inches from his. She felt soft all over like cotton and wind and meadows. He looked down at her beautiful eyes and parted lips, and caught his breath.

Her hand slid up to his chin and its unkempt growth of whiskers. Her fingers tickled the stubble as she smiled.

His heart was pounding so loud he was certain she could hear it. He was frozen with her in his arms, unable to move or take his gaze from her lovely face. As if she were Polly.

Then she slid her hand to his neck, pulling his head down. He felt the velvet softness of her lips on his. His whole life welled up inside him. For a moment, the world spun around him. How he wanted to hold her and tell her about his lost love, his face in her silky hair as he wept. But he couldn't move.

Then she drew back with a sweet smile. 'That was for saving my life, Chance Darringer.'

He swallowed hard, watching her slide from his arms and get to her feet. She backed away, still smiling down at him. Then she turned and curled up wearily near her sister. She snuggled close to Becky, the dog between them, its gaze still fixed on Chance.

Chance's face burned. He stood up to take a walk in the darkness. He still had trouble breathing. How he had longed to hold Polly that way! Their hesitant kiss in her doorway, his arms frozen at his side, had been all he could carry back to Texas. Now Polly was gone.

Chance leaned on his buckskin stallion and stared up at the stars. He liked the land. Riding free in the saddle. Smelling the sweet night air. Crossing the desert with the sage turned silver and the cacti in bloom. Feeling his stallion's great muscles move beneath him. Camping at night with the sky full of glistening stars.

Yet something had been missing from his life. Polly had been the unexpected answer. He had gone loco in Texas and had to return, had to ask for her hand. Now she was dead, and he was alone and bitter and out for revenge. One of these men had to be the killer.

Chance would have no rest until he found the right man. He'd follow them all the way to Antler and the Rawlins's ranch. Sooner or later, the man would give himself away. Somehow, Chance would smoke him out.

If the man didn't get him first.

2

The next morning, Chance awoke to the smell of frying bacon. He was too hungry to chastise Grimey for making a fire, and joined the group for breakfast. Susanna was a wonderful cook, but Oscar's sour disposition managed to spoil some of the pleasure. He never left Susanna's side, pointedly showing his possession of her.

'Chance is gonna ride with us a ways,' Grimey said.

Oscar grunted. 'We can use another gun. But I ain't payin'.'

Susanna looked stricken by his remark. She quickly looked at Chance, who merely shrugged. It was obvious she thought Oscar ungrateful.

On the trail to the northwest, the country became more rugged. Chance rode with Grimey and Tolliver, listening to their tales. He had little to say to Oscar, as a mutual dislike simmered between them. Lynch and Borcher never spoke to anyone if they could help it. Often, Susanna's delightful humor was the only reason to smile.

Sometimes Tolliver would sing trail songs, his deep, throaty voice carrying in the night. Many of the songs he sang were sad and wistful. One night, the cowhand tried to be more cheerful and sang a lively tune. Susanna sang along with him, her voice sweet and clear.

Sad, Chance stared into the night. He could wait no longer. Somehow, he had to flush out the killer.

He soon managed to get a poker game started. Becky was asleep and Susanna was hunched by the fireside a few feet away. All the men sat in to ease their boredom, even Oscar, who was pretty stingy. Grimey was half on guard, half in the game. And sooner or later, each one of them pulled out a Rocking R money clip when they were digging for coin.

Chance was suffering, his mind in turmoil. Grimey had been right. They all had the clips. He had no way of knowing who had lost one. He folded his cards.

'You got law in Antler?'

'Not anymore,' Grimey said. 'We had a sheriff, but he got shot in the back last year. No one wants the job.'

The game continued. After a while, Chance drew out the money clip with the greenback in it. He let the gold flash in the firelight.

'Where'd you get that?' Lynch asked.

'Back in Tombstone.'

Lynch dealt the cards. 'You steal it or win it?'

'It was alongside a dying woman. She was beaten pretty bad, but she was still alive when I found her. She was able to talk some before she died.'

His words hung in the air like a heavy cloud. Part of it was a lie, but he had to get their attention. Yet he saw no fearful reactions. No one jumped up with gun

34

in hand. Their faces were like stone.

'You know who did it?' Borcher asked.

'Got me a notion,' Chance said.

Lynch glared at him. 'You tryin' to say it's one of us?'

'We all played poker in Tombstone,' Borcher cut in. 'I lost one of those clips myself, tryin' to draw on an inside straight. But I can't recall the faces at the table.'

'Yeah, you told me about that,' Lynch said. 'Reckon you're dead in the water, Darringer.'

'Maybe not. Any one of you could have done it. And you pulled out the mornin' after it happened.'

Borcher grunted. 'You gonna draw cards or not?'

Chance looked at Oscar, who was busy rolling a cigarette. His hands were not trembling. There was a long, dead quiet. Chance waited, heart pounding, sweat on his face.

The tension was heavy, loud in the stillness.

Grimey looked stunned. 'Chance, that's too bad. Did you know her?'

'I wanted to marry her.'

He turned in his cards and stood up, heading for the nearby rocks. He wrapped his arms about himself. He felt as if he would collapse. His face was hot in the chill of night. His heart hurt so bad he thought it would crumble right in his chest.

Suddenly, he felt a soft hand on his arm. He stiffened as he turned. Susanna gazed up at him with tears brimming in her eyes. She looked sad and beautiful in the starlight.

'Chance, I'm so sorry.'

At first, he wanted to hold her so that she would hold him and ease his pain. But then he felt sudden anger that she wasn't Polly. He couldn't speak and turned his back to her. Hurting, he waited for her to move away. He felt bad that he had offended her, but she didn't know how lovely she looked. Nor how lovely Polly had been.

But Susanna didn't move away. She

touched his arm again, pulling at his sleeve until he turned to look down at her. They were alone in the starlight. No one was looking for them. He gazed down at the tears in her eyes.

'Chance, everyone has a right to cry.'

He couldn't stop himself. He slid his arms around her and held her to him, pressing her face to his chest. Her arms went gently around his waist. He buried his face in her soft hair. For a long while they stood silently. His eyes were wet, but the full flow of tears remained buried in his heart.

She lifted her face from his chest. She looked so beautiful in the pale light, so like Polly. He couldn't help himself. He bent his head and pressed his lips to hers. She kissed him back with a tenderness that nearly broke his heart.

Then he released her. She stepped back with a hesitant smile. 'If you ever need a friend, Chance, I'm here.'

She turned and walked away. He

could still feel her in his arms. He looked toward the campfire. No one had seen them.

He didn't sleep well that night. He could be killed in his sleep, a knife at his throat. He could be shot in the back or pushed into the river. He knew that whoever tried would be the killer.

Yet nothing happened for the next two days. No one mentioned the money clip. The men watched him, but said nothing. The killer would be wondering just what Polly said before she died. Chance would have to be silenced, sooner or later.

Susanna was especially nice to Chance, giving him extra helpings and more biscuits than the others. Oscar didn't seem to notice, but his dislike for Chance was obvious.

When they reached the pass, they were in a forest where pines and aspen crowded the slopes. Snow lay in patches above them. The river was twenty feet wide and blue, its deep, violent rapids glistening with white foam at every turn.

Most of the way, there was an easy trail along the west bank. Sometimes, they rode up into the pines, where the air was cool and clean. The extra horses and pack mule were always between Tolliver and Grimey. The dog trailed Chance, but wouldn't allow him to come near.

Their first night in the pass, they camped along the river near a twenty-foot drop to the water. Susanna cooked biscuits and beans. Chance raved about the biscuits, which were fluffy and hot and tasty. Becky sneaked him an extra one.

'Susanna won't have to cook when we're married,' Oscar bragged. 'We got us a woman doin' the cookin' and cleanin'.'

'Mighty shame,' Chance said.

Oscar glared at him. 'Reckon you'll be headin' north for Montana when we get through the pass.'

'No, I'll be headin' for Antler. Sooner

or later, one of you is gonna make a mistake.'

'You're a fool,' Oscar said. 'The killer's probably wandering around Tombstone right now. Or he's down in Mexico. While you're hangin' around us, he's gettin' away.'

Grimey changed the subject quickly. Then Tolliver began to tell some of his tall tales to entertain Becky. It was later that Chance began to tell his own stories, partly to disarm them and keep them off guard.

'When my twin brother and I were twelve, our Uncle Zed took us on a drive north to Missouri. Afterward, we went to Springfield because Zed knew Wild Bill Hickok. We saw that Hickok was over six feet and wore two pistols. He had a big sombrero. But, funny enough, he was pigeon-toed.'

'You're a liar,' Lynch said.

Chance slowly turned from where he sat. He looked up at Lynch, who was standing some ten feet from the fire. The man was asking for trouble and looked plenty dangerous.

Everyone fell silent. Chance felt hot down to his boots, yet his fingers were cold. Slowly, without his hands touching the ground, he got to his feet. He didn't look at anyone but Lynch as he left the campfire and the circle of people.

Lynch stood waiting. There was no smile on his face, not even a leer. His nearly closed left eye was red. His good eye squinted in the moonlight. The thin line of his mouth turned down at the edges. He wore a six-gun low on his right hip. There was a knife at his belt. His body was strong and hard with great muscles in his arms and shoulders.

'Darringer, you're a liar. I saw Hickok. He never looked like that.'

'You're mistaken, Lynch.'

'Mr. Lynch to you, sonny.'

The fight was a setup, Chance knew. Either Lynch was the killer or someone had paid him to go after Chance. From the corner of his eye, he saw the dog stand up, hair raised on its haunches.

Lynch advanced a step. They stood facing each other in the moonlight. The noise of the river was deafening. Chance felt the others staring at them, but he didn't take his eyes off Lynch.

Chance couldn't back down. He had a feeling the money clip and Polly's 'last words' were the reason for the challenge. He had to fight. And maybe, just maybe, Lynch was his man. They dropped their gun belts.

Lynch moved forward another step. Suddenly, he rushed. Chance ducked and sidestepped. Lynch caught himself and spun around, and charged again.

Chance shoved his fist in the man's hard belly, almost breaking his arm. Lynch grabbed him by the neck with both hands. Chance brought his knee up into the man's middle and shoved him back. He grabbed Lynch's neck with one hand and pounded his jaw with the other. They clinched.

Barely able to breathe, Chance fought free. Furious, he gasped for air and charged, pounding the man right and left, over and over, beating him mercilessly with his fists. Lynch tried to fight back, but kept reeling from the blows.

Finally Lynch was on his hands and knees. Chance drew back a step. Suddenly, Lynch pulled a knife from his boot and sprang to his feet, the blade level in his grasp, pointing at Chance as he advanced.

'I'm gonna gut you, sonny.'

Lynch was dazed but determined to kill. Chance dodged the first slash of the knife. The man kept charging. Chance sidestepped and danced as the knife kept at him. Once the blade cut Chance's left forearm as he jumped back.

Chance was perilously near the edge of the river-bank, and he had to do something fast. He faked dizziness, grabbing his bleeding arm as if in pain, and his legs buckled.

Lynch darted in for the kill, and Chance jumped aside.

Losing his balance and unable to stop his charge, Lynch spun out into midair. Legs and arms flying, he seemed suspended in space for just a second. He didn't yell as he went plunging down toward the water some twenty feet below.

Chance turned to look down. Lynch had landed in the river and was fighting to get to shore. He looked like a water bug, his arms and legs kicking in every direction. Oscar and Grimey came to stand on either side of Chance as they gazed down at Lynch, who had crawled onto the rocks below. He had lost his knife. He was beaten. Resting, he glared up at them with his one good eye. He was one mad hombre. Grimey went down the steep bank to help him.

Oscar turned to look at Chance in the moonlight. No one else could hear his cold, pointed words.

'You were lucky this time, Darringer.'

Chance turned slowly, his eyes gleaming with fury. Oscar just smiled, looked down at Grimey and Lynch, and turned away. The attack could have been Oscar's idea. Now Chance was certain he had their attention. They weren't sure how much he knew, how much Polly might have said.

Chance watched Oscar stroll back to the campfire, where the others waited. Grimey half carried Lynch back up the embankment and left him with Oscar. Then he came over and gave Chance his gun belt, which Chance buckled on. He also brought a canteen and helped wash and wrap Chance's arm.

'You were plenty lucky,' he said. 'Lynch is a mean one. He ain't gonna forget this, so watch yourself. Maybe you should head on without us.'

'I ain't leavin' until I get the killer.'

'But Oscar's right. He could still be in Tombstone.'

'That ain't what Polly said.' He turned away. He was hurting pretty bad. And he trusted Grimey, but not enough to admit Polly had said nothing. He had to keep the question open.

When they got back to the campfire, everyone was asleep but Tolliver, who was on guard. Chance, his arm hurting, rolled into his blankets. He lay staring at the flames. His pain was more than the knife wound. He was getting nowhere.

★ ★ ★

The next morning, they continued their ride along the river. The trail had narrowed to barely three feet wide and climbed high above the water. It was a dangerous path with an eighty-foot drop straight down a rocky wall. The sky was overcast, the rising wind cold and cutting to the bone.

The rapids below looked icy and deep. The river was barely twenty feet across as it fought its way through the pass. Patches of snow hung from the trees above. Brush and rocks scratched at the riders.

Susanna guided her black mare along the rough trail behind Tolliver, with

Chance following. The others were ahead with the pack mule and spare horses, behind the trotting dog that led the way. All were riding very carefully, single file. Chance liked the way Susanna sat in the saddle, tall and easy.

Suddenly, her mare shied at something in the brush on their left. The animal swung sideways, lost its footing, and plunged into the open air. Then it squealed and went crashing down toward the river. Susanna cried out, trying to stay in the saddle.

The mare skidded straight down through the scattering rocks, twisted its right foreleg, then rolled on its side, as Susanna tried to jump free. But they fell all the way into the rocks and rapids. Stunned, Susanna was thrown into the rushing water and swept downriver, struggling to keep her head up.

Chance didn't hesitate. He rode his buckskin right down the terrible drop through the rocks and brush. The stallion slid most of the way on its rump, stones and dirt flying around them. At any moment they could plunge to their death. But the big buckskin never lost its balance.

When they hit the water's edge, he reined about, pulling his rope to swing a wide loop. He couldn't see her. She was probably underwater, out of sight. The roar of the rapids was deafening.

He forced his stallion into the water. They were swept like sticks through the dangerous rocks, fighting to stay upright. He kept his rope in hand, but his mount was out of control. He jumped off and let the animal swim to the bank. The icy water drained him of all feeling.

Swept downriver by the terrible flood of water, Susanna was still out of sight. Then he saw floating golden-brown hair in the rocks ahead near the east bank. Terrified she had drowned, he fought his way over to the scene, hooking his rope around his shoulder and under his arm.

Grabbing for her under the water, he seized a part of her skirt, then her arm. He yanked and pulled until she was free of the debris. He jerked her head out of the water. She was unconscious and deathly white.

His arm around her waist, he turned in the freezing river. Through the white spray, he saw one of the men fifty feet above on the trail on the far side. It was Tolliver on his bay. The cowhand had managed to turn around or back his horse all the way down the narrow path.

Unable to make it across to the other side of the river. Chance dragged Susanna as best he could around the rocks and over to the east bank. It took all his remaining strength to get her out of the water. Gasping for breath, he rolled her over on her stomach and put pressure on her back. Then he turned her again. She lay staring up at him, fighting for air.

He sat her up and bent her over his knee, rocking her. She coughed and choked and gasped. He didn't know what else to do. He kept pressing on her back.

'I'm all right,' she gasped.

He allowed her to roll back to the wet dirt. She lay on her elbow, fighting for breath and shaking her head. Her hair looked black as it lay across her face and throat. She was soaked clean through and looked sickly pale. He, too, was frozen.

Tolliver shouted to them, but Chance couldn't hear him over the rapids. The man was pointing downriver. Chance remembered there was some clear water farther on, where the river widened. He scooped the cold, shivering woman up in his arms. Her head rolled against his shoulder, and a white hand slid up his chest to cling to his jacket.

Exhausted but determined, Chance walked downstream along the east bank. He could see his buckskin on the far side, trailing and tossing its head. The animal finally met with

Tolliver as the trail came back down to the bank.

The river was much wider and more shallow, but the water was still white and forceful, maybe six feet deep. Chance lowered Susanna to the ground. After shouting instructions over the river's roar, Tolliver attached a rope to an aspen's trunk and flung it over to Chance, who tied it to a rock on his side.

Chance then made his rope into a sling for Susanna, and attached it to Tolliver's with loops. He threw the rest of the rope across so the cowhand could pull her over. Before they started to move her, she turned to Chance where they both knelt on the bank. She was so pale and cold, he feared she would die.

She reached up to touch his face. 'Thank you,' she whispered.

He swallowed hard as he helped her into the sling. She gripped the rough ropes with her soft fingers. Thrown over the water, she cried out in fear but held on. She dangled so low her feet dragged in the water, but, at last, she was across.

As Susanna reached Tolliver's grasp, Chance plunged into the icy river and pulled himself across, hand over hand on the rope. His palms burned.

As Chance crawled onto the west bank, Tolliver was already wrapping Susanna in his blankets. Chance asked him how he had been able to get back to them on the narrow ledge.

'My horse will back anywhere I tell it,' the man said. 'The others had to go find a place to turn around. I told 'em not to come back so we wouldn't meet 'em on the trail.'

'That took a heap of courage.'

'You get to be my age,' the white-bearded man said, 'and courage is just hard work and common sense.'

The buckskin stallion shook itself, trying to get dry. Susanna was shivering but standing. Tolliver stood up as they retrieved their ropes.

'We gotta get up ahead to the clearing

so we can build a fire,' he said. 'I figured the others would have sense enough not to come back. But there he is.'

A rider galloped up. It was Oscar Rawlins on his sorrel. If they had met him on that ledge, it would have been a disaster. He rode down from the trail to where the trio waited by the bank. He dismounted, frantic, and knelt by Susanna. His hard face actually looked worried as he stroked her cold cheeks.

'Are you all right?'

'Yes. Chance saved me.'

Grumbling his thanks, Oscar stood up. 'Well, the others are makin' camp ahead. You can ride with me, Susanna.'

'It's not safe,' Chance said. 'She can ride my horse. I'll walk.'

So it was that Susanna was lifted bodily by Chance and set astride on the saddle. She smiled down at him, but her lips were quivering. The stallion obeyed Chance's touch and stood quiet. Taking the reins, Chance led the animal behind Oscar and in front of Tolliver.

It seemed forever as they followed the narrow path. When they reached the spot where Susanna had fallen, Chance looked back. She had no color and was frightened, hunched over in the saddle and gripping the pommel. He himself was wet and cold to the bone.

He prayed that the others would not turn back and meet them on the narrow ledge. But he soon learned that only Oscar had taken that chance.

When they reached a clearing surrounded by aspens and away from the river, they saw a blazing fire. Becky came running to meet them and anxiously watched as Chance lowered Susanna. Holding her a moment in his arms, Chance hesitated. Her head against his chest, he savored the moment, but he wasn't thinking of her. Then he carried her to the fire.

He was glad he had saved her. Nothing was going to happen to Susanna while he was around. One dead woman was enough.

Tolliver made a makeshift tent of blankets between the trees. With Becky's help, Susanna changed there into dry clothes. She was still trembling as she came to kneel by the fire. She wore a green dress with a dark-green jacket. Oscar draped several blankets around her. Becky snuggled against her. The dog curled up and lay on Susanna's feet.

Soaked through himself, Chance used the tent to change into his one other shirt and Levi's. He poured water out of his boots, but put them back on. Then he pulled on his old wool coat and lay his wet leather jacket along with his other clothes by the fire on some brambles. He cleaned and oiled his weapons. Tolliver was doing a passable job of warming up the beans and making coffee.

Suddenly, Susanna fainted, rolling to her side.

Chance jumped up and ran to her before Oscar could react. Kneeling and straightening her legs, Chance slapped and rubbed her limbs through the blankets. Becky, frightened, began to help. He gently slapped Susanna's cold face. Her eyes flickered open, but she looked dazed. He and Becky worked on her frantically.

He couldn't bear to see another woman die.

The other men watched, helpless. The dog licked Susanna's face. Night was falling fast. It was going to be terribly cold. Chance felt no warmth in her. He rubbed her hands and legs until his arms nearly fell from him.

Finally, color returned to her cheeks. Her eyes opened, and she became more alert. Becky cried with relief. Chance sat back on his heels and took Susanna's hands in his, rubbing them. Tears trickled down her cheeks.

'I thought I was dying,' she said.

Oscar came to kneel near her, shoving Chance aside. He seized her hands. 'Well, you look all right now.'

After a moment of rubbing her

hands, Oscar kissed her fingers and looked truly distressed and concerned. She smiled at him.

But Oscar's true nature surfaced a short time later. 'That was a fool thing to do back there, Susanna,' he said sharply. 'Weren't you watching the trail?'

She stared at him. 'Yes, but there was something in the brush. A lizard or snake.'

'Well, a good mare is dead back there. We were gonna raise colts with her.'

'I'm sorry,' she said, still staring at him.

Chance stalked away from them, fury building within him. He could barely keep from attacking the man. Susanna seemed surprised too, but soon she smiled and made a joke about the coffee.

Chance turned on his heel, anger burning his face. He walked over to the water's edge, drawing his coat tightly about him. He was cold himself, but he was too angry to think about it. He welcomed the roar of the river.

Grimey walked over to him and asked, 'You all right, Chance?'

'I'm thinkin' I won't like Antler.'

'Why not?'

'Because I might have to kill that man. And if I can't find a reason, I'm gonna be mighty sorry.'

'You might be sorry anyhow if you go to Antler. Somethin' bad is going on there. Silas had more men than he needs. Some are plenty mean. He's got three fancy guns hangin' around too. And there's been a lot of night ridin'. Ranchers and farmers have all been hit — some folks were even killed trying to fight back.'

'You got proof it was Silas?'

'No, but some of his men got a lot of spendin' money.'

'And it's over land?'

'Well, yeah. But I got me an idea that if Silas had the whole valley, he'd find reason for more killin'. It's a feelin' of power, I reckon.'

'So why do you stay?'

'I was gonna jump ship at Tombstone. Then I met Miss Susanna and the little girl. I got worried about them.'

'She gonna marry Oscar for sure?'

'Like I said, she and Becky got no blood kin. Her ma had a brother back East, but they figure he died a long time ago. All they got is the Rawlinses.'

Grimey knelt to look down at the glistening, violent water as he continued. 'She told me she was ten when her ma was dyin' with a newborn in her arms. Susanna sat right there as her mother begged her to marry Oscar someday and look after Becky. Susanna made that promise with her pa lookin' on.'

Grimey paused to glance toward camp, his voice lower. 'I figure their pa wasn't good for much. Their ma knew the Rawlinses had a lot of money. She couldn't rest in peace not knowin' how her girls would be provided for. And six years after she was gone, I'm guessin' their pa got some money for makin' the deal. Right after he sent her picture to the Rawlinses.'

Chance made a face, his hands shoved in his coat pockets. Grimey's words didn't make things any easier. But the big man shrugged as he stood up. He could see that Chance was irritated.

'Look, Chance, maybe Oscar ain't so bad. I don't know for sure that he's been mixed up in the night raids. And maybe he talks the way he does because he don't know how to talk to women. Maybe he can't say he was worried about her.'

Chance could understand that. He didn't know how to talk to women, either. They never reacted to anything in a way he expected. He looked north in the moonlight. He suddenly felt the weariness of his body, the exhaustion of his misery.

'How long before we get through the pass?'

Grimey shrugged. 'One more night

in here, I reckon. Then it's a couple of nights to Antler and a long ride to the ranch.'

Chance went back to the campfire, with Grimey following. He saw Susanna asleep where she sat with her head on Oscar's shoulder. His arm was still around her. He looked at Chance with smug arrogance. Becky was asleep in her blankets near them, the dog against her feet.

Chance bent down to pet the animal. It snarled and snapped at his hand. He drew back quickly. Grimey laughed and Tolliver shook his head, amused.

'You know how wolves are,' Tolliver said. 'They just keep followin' their prey till the time is right. I figure he's got his sights set on you, Chance.'

Grimey chuckled. 'Now, that could be it, all right.'

Rolling into his blankets and ignoring their fun, Chance decided the dog would be better off with Becky and Susanna anyway. It would have a home and maybe a chance to get over its distrust. But he would miss the animal. He felt a kinship with it.

When Chance awakened at first light, Susanna was dressed in her riding clothes and cooking breakfast. Oscar, Lynch, and Tolliver were asleep, Grimey was on guard down by the river, and Becky was still curled up with the dog. It was cold and damp. He moved closer to the fire.

'You look all right,' he said, sitting near where Susanna knelt. She smiled and poured him fresh coffee.

'I want to thank you. You saved my life again.'

'I took a fool chance.'

'Are you sorry?'

He managed to grin. 'Not a bit.'

'Are you going to Antler with us?'

'Look, it ain't none of my business, but — '

Oscar's voice cut in as he tossed aside his blankets.

'You're right, Darringer. It ain't none of your business.'

Susanna started at Oscar's rudeness,

then smiled and poured him some coffee. Oscar glared at Chance, who glared back. Growing hatred passed between the two men like flashes of lightning. She spoke quickly.

'Oscar says it's really beautiful country around Antler — right at the foot of the mountains, with a lot of ranches. He says there's elk and antelope and wild turkeys.' Her light words defused the tension.

Becky sat up, yawning. Borcher and Lynch came over to have their breakfast. Lynch's good eye narrowed as he looked at Chance. It was obvious they were not finished with each other.

After breaking camp, the party spent the day in the saddle, with Susanna riding Hutch's horse. They spent another night along the river in a grove of cottonwoods. Chance knew they'd be in the open come morning. He spent a lot of time looking at Susanna, glad she was alive and well. Becky was chattering more than usual.

'Oscar says I get my own room, Chance. All to myself. And a pony. I get my own pony.'

'A pinto,' Oscar promised.

Chance watched grimly as Oscar turned on the charm. He was making promises to Susanna as well. She would have her own cook and maid. He would find her a new mount and have a handmade saddle ordered for her. Once a year, he would take her to a big city. She could have new clothes any time she desired, and rosewood furniture.

Susanna listened and smiled. Chance gritted his teeth. He knew that under Oscar's forced charm was a mean, cruel person. He could smell the depravity. He hated the thought of this man putting his hands on a woman like Susanna. On any woman. He didn't sleep easy.

In the morning, they broke camp again and followed the river. By noon they were in the verdant open land. The plains rolled as far as they could see to the north, east, and west. To the south of the road were green foothills and white-crested mountains. Overhead, a golden eagle soared faster than the wind, its cry lingering long after it was gone.

'I'll see you in Antler,' Chance told the group. 'I want to look at the valley some.'

He didn't tell them he needed time alone. His grief had not been resolved. He was bitter and angry, his pain clouding his mind. If he wanted to get the right man and still survive, he had to have his senses.

Oscar herded the group ahead of Chance, who sat watching them leave. Grimey turned in the saddle to wave, as did Susanna and Becky. Chance watched them ride into the aspens and disappear from sight. The dog trailed them.

Suddenly weary, he turned his buckskin north across the rolling hills. As he rode, he saw cattle in every direction. There were isolated ranches. A hanging tree with dangling rope. Some lonely graves along the trail.

The road to Antler grew more distant behind him.

The first night out, he sat by the fire, grim with thoughts of Antler and the Rawlins ranch. Suddenly he heard a sound and sensed movement. He jumped to one knee, six-guns in both hands.

The black, wolflike dog wandered into the firelight. It lay down, yellow eyes fixed on Chance.

'Well, so you came home.'

The animal didn't make a sound. Chance was tickled. He threw it a chunk of jerky. It chewed on it without taking its eyes from Chance, then, satisfied, it rested its head on its paws and went to sleep. Grinning, Chance poured himself another cup of coffee. He was glad of the company.

★ ★ ★

While Chance was sitting by his campfire with the aloof dog, Oscar's outfit arrived at the Rocking R ranch. They rode through rocks, clumps of brush, stately aspens, and chunky cottonwoods until they reached a rise overlooking a wide clearing where the buildings and corrals were spread.

Moonlight shone in the cold and silent night as they rode down the slope and over to the hitching rail in front of the house. Susanna slid from the saddle. She was weary and sore. Becky swung down beside her. A ranch hand approached and carried their carpetbags into the house, then slipped away to care for the horses and mule.

Standing outside the big, rambling house, Susanna hesitated. Oscar took her arm and led her to the door, shoving it open.

She was surprised at the lavish furnishings. Everything was made of rich, dark wood and plush upholstery. The draperies looked expensive, all fringe and green velvet. The carpet was deep and soft. A fire burned in

67

a great stone hearth, over which hung graceful elk horns.

A man by the fire stood up, rubbing sleep from his eyes. He was in his sixties and stocky like Oscar. He had white hair and a white mustache trimmed away from a wide, thin mouth. His eyes were pale gray. He wore a smoking jacket of red velvet, and held a pipe in his hand.

'Oscar, you're back. And this must be Susanna and Becky.'

Silas Rawlins stared at Susanna, never having expected she was even more beautiful than her picture. He hugged her and Becky. Oscar set their luggage aside and tossed his saddlebags on the corner desk near the large gun case. Susanna went to warm her hands by the fire.

'You must be exhausted,' Silas said. 'Oscar, take them to their rooms. See that they're fed. Then come back and talk with me.'

Neither Susanna nor Becky wanted anything to eat. They were too weary.

Becky was given a small but comfortable room, which she loved. Susanna was led down the hallway to her own room. Oscar set her luggage just inside the door, as she didn't move farther to allow him entrance. He stood looking at her.

'You'd better be settin' the date. My pa don't have much patience,' he said.

Uneasy, she nodded. 'But I need time, Oscar.'

He put his hands on her slim arms. She tensed. He drew her to him and crushed her lips with his. The kiss was long and forceful, showing his demand for dominance.

Frantically, she thought of Chance and wished he were here instead, wished that circumstances were different and that Chance wasn't in mourning, that he was thinking of her, wanting to see her again. Yet it was all so hopeless. She was trapped.

When Oscar released her, she was out of breath. Yet she managed to back away with a smile.

'Good night, Oscar.'

'Maybe I'm a little rough, but you know I ain't much around women. I've been in the saddle most of my life. You gotta understand that.'

She relaxed now, her smile genuine. 'We just need a little time, Oscar. Everything will be all right.'

'You bet, honey. I want to make you the finest lady in this valley.'

He turned back down the hallway as she closed the door. Inside, she told herself anxiously that she had made the right decision. She was taking care of Becky. They would have a home, just as her mother had wanted. And if they could survive living in squalor and being dragged from camp to camp, they could survive whatever was ahead.

Oscar stood and glared at the closed door. He knew his time would come, so he turned back down the hallway. When he reached the hearth, Silas was filling his pipe. They sat in chairs facing each other. Silas nodded at the saddlebags.

'Any trouble with collectin' for the cattle?'

'Nope. Got eighteen dollars a head.'

'Them miners must be pretty hungry.'

Oscar nodded. 'Did you get the Crandall place?'

'That old man is plenty stubborn. He's already lost two hands from a raid. The other one quit. That means he's all by himself with two hundred head. And we've already scattered his herd up into the brush country.'

'Should be easy pickings.'

'We'll just take our time, slow and easy. I figure by the end of the next two years, we'll own the whole valley and half of Antler. I just lent a lot of money to Bragg, the man who runs the general store. Pretty soon nobody will get supplies unless I say so.'

Oscar smiled. 'What do you think of Susanna?'

'Mighty pretty. I figure we made a good bargain. We'd better keep quiet about that fat trust fund her ma's brother left for her. She might figure she don't need the likes of you.'

'How would she find out? You got them papers locked up in the safe. When she's twenty-one, it's all hers. And mine. But we gotta be married before then. And her birthday's in July.'

Silas grunted. 'Ain't nothin' gonna stop it. She thinks she's penniless. If her pa hadn't asked us to deal with that lawyer, we'd never have known about it. We're lucky her old man was a fool.'

'That's a heap of money she's gettin'.' Oscar yawned lazily. 'I'm a lucky man.'

Silas filled his pipe with smelly tobacco.

'Listen, Pa, we lost Hutch. Some Apache hit us at a water hole. Then a fellow came along for the fight. He stayed and rode through the pass with us. And he took on Lynch — beat the devil out of him.'

'Takes a lot of man to do that. Who is he?'

'Chance Darringer.'

Silas frowned. 'A gunfighter.'

'Yeah. Wears two guns. Thinks he's tough.'

'Is he still here?'

'No, he's out wandering around somewhere.'

'Too bad. We coulda used him.'

'Not likely. He shows his face around here, I may have to end up shootin' him myself. Some woman was killed down in Tombstone. He found one of our money clips with her. He's been accusin' every one of us.'

Silas leaned back in surprise. 'You figure it was Borcher or Lynch?'

'No, I figure the killer's still down there. Borcher lost one of his clips in a card game down in Tombstone. But this Darringer, he's like a wolf, doggin' our trail.'

'Well, let him. We got work to do.'

They sat talking long into the night.

★ ★ ★

Off in the hills, Chance tossed and turned in his blankets near his campfire. Come morning, he sat up suddenly, gun in hand. A movement had awakened him, but it was only the dog. The animal had moved closer, lying next to his boot and watching him with gleaming yellow eyes.

'You sure like to sneak around. Maybe that's what I ought to call you. Sneak.'

The animal raised its head and snarled.

'Well, all right. I reckon that's not very dignified. I'll call you Pardner.'

With that, the animal rested its head on its paws.

Chance enjoyed the animal's company as he rode the valley. It was still wide-open cattle country. None of the ranches had more than a few hundred head, mostly longhorn steer or cows with calves. Barbed-wire fences, which he hated, were many miles apart, but there were frequent gates.

One morning, Chance sat poking his campfire with a stick. He hadn't found peace, but he was finally in control of his fury. He looked up at the sky, where a black vulture sailed with the wind, then over at his buckskin stallion. The animal's powerful muscles rippled as it pawed the earth and shook its black mane and tail. Chance gazed at the watchful wolf-dog. He knew it was time to head for Antler.

Chance broke camp, then saddled and mounted his stallion. He decided to cut due west to see the rest of the valley on the way to Antler. The dog trailed.

He spent another night under the stars. In the morning he continued due west toward some brush country that poked up beyond the rolling green hills.

Before noon, he passed through a gate in a barbed-wire fence. He rode farther through the scattered pines. Abruptly, he reined to a halt. The dog had stopped, hair raised on the back of its neck. Chance sniffed the air. Smoke. Slowly, he rode forward through the trees. Aspens whispered at him. The pines smelled unusually pungent.

When he came over the next hill, he saw the smoldering ruins of a small ranch house in a far clearing. Only the stone chimney still stood. The corrals around a barn that had collapsed from fire were empty. Four loose horses grazed up in the grove of trees. One was nickering to his stallion, breaking the deadly silence.

The dog ran back and forth, nervous and snarling. Chance saw no sign of life.

Suddenly, a shot rang out. The bullet whistled past his ear, singeing the skin of his neck.

3

As the bullet whistled past his ear, Chance spun his buckskin about and galloped into the trees. He leaned low in the saddle, six-gun in his right hand, reins in his left. He saw no sign of life. The dog was hunched over in the grass.

Then Chance saw the sunlight dance on a rifle barrel in the brush behind the house. He could only guess it was the owner.

'Hello, the house,' Chance shouted. 'I'm a stranger.'

His voice echoed in the stillness. At long last, a husky voice called back to him, 'Then show yourself.'

Holstering his weapon, Chance rode from the trees. There was sweat on his face and his breath was tight. The man could plug him dead center. The dog trotted ahead. He rode near the ruins and reined up.

At length, an old man came out of the brush, rifle in hand. He was short, wiry, gray whiskered, and lame in his right leg. His eyes were black and beady. White hair was thick on his head. As he walked forward, he kept his Winchester aimed at Chance.

'What do you want here?'

'Thought you might need help.'

The old man grunted and lowered his rifle. 'Shoulda been here last night. When I come back from town around midnight, it was too late. The whole place had gone up in smoke. Lots of riders tracked in and out.'

'Mind if I water my horse?'

'Sure. Over by the corrals.'

Chance rode over to the trough, the old man walking along with him. The dog hit the water's edge before the horse, lapping it up noisily.

The man frowned. 'Looks half wolf.'

'Probably is. He don't bark none. And he don't wag his tail. Snarls a lot, though.' Chance dismounted and allowed his horse to drink a little at a time. 'What happened here?'

'Rawlins. Can't be nobody else. He's been tryin' to buy me out. Killed two of my hands one night. The other got scared and quit. Night riders scattered my herd. I got a couple hundred head runnin' wild up in the brush and probably losin' some calves. Now they burned me out.'

'Sorry to see it.'

'By the way, my name's Max Crandall.'

Chance held out his hand. 'Chance Darringer.'

The old man hesitated. 'No foolin'?'

They shook hands as Chance nodded, then put his head under the pump and doused himself with water. It felt good. Then he sat on the edge of the big trough and wiped his face with his bandanna. The sun was warm and caressing.

'So you're one of them Darringers.'

'Yeah, but I'm really just a cowhand.'

'I can use a good hand. And your name. Might scare off them night riders. How about it?'

Chance studied him a moment. He liked the old man. Chance wasn't afraid of night riders. In fact, he hadn't learned how to be afraid of anything or anyone. And he needed a home until he could find the killer. It would be a good cover as well.

'First I gotta ride into Antler and check on a few things. After that, sure. What's the pay?'

'How about ten percent of what I get from the Army?'

'Well, I sure hope I'm worth it.'

'You can prove it about now, son.'

Chance followed the old man's gaze. Three riders were approaching. They were slick-looking men in fancy dark shirts, wearing hats decorated with conchos and feathers. They rode high-stepping horses with tooled saddles, and their fancy gun belts held shiny six-guns.

The man facing them on the left was the tallest. He had a hard, swarthy face that bore a sleazy smile.

The old man had his rifle aimed at his gut.

'Mr. Crandall, my name is Hadley. Looks like you've had some trouble here,' the tall man said.

'What do you want?'

'Mr. Rawlins asked me to ride by and see if you've been thinking about his offer.'

'You tell Rawlins I ain't interested. Not now. Not tomorrow. Not any time. He can take his offer and choke on it.'

Hadley leaned on the pommel of his saddle. 'Now, Mr. Crandall, be reasonable. Maybe I can get Mr. Rawlins to up his price a little.'

'I ain't sellin'. I got a herd to bring in.'

'You and this stranger? Maybe you oughta tell him what a risk he's taking just being here.'

'This here's my new hand, Chance Darringer.'

The words hung heavily in the air. Hadley straightened, surprised for just a moment. Then his smile turned crooked. His dark eyes gleamed as he pushed back his hat with his left hand and rested his right on the edge of the pommel. His voice was mocking.

'So what's in a name? Nothing, my friend.'

Chance just stood calmly and casually, a faint smile on his face.

'Let's take him,' the man in the middle said. 'It would sure please Mr. Rawlins.' He looked sinister, his blue eyes pale in his dark face.

Hadley shook his head. 'No, Parsons, this is a friendly visit. Mr. Darringer, this other fellow here is Mr. Snow. Reckon you heard of us.'

Chance shook his head. Hadley's smile faded as he spoke.

'Mr. Crandall, you had better think this over.'

At that moment Parsons stepped down from his horse. His dark face and high cheekbones made him look even more sinister. Gleaming eyes narrowed as he moved away from the others.

'So you're a Darringer. I always wanted one of 'em notched on my six-shooter.'

Chance was not an experienced gunfighter, but he was plenty fast. He had backed men down before. It had been a challenge and some kind of dangerous fun. But that fun seemed like a hundred years ago. And now it was obvious that Parsons was not going to back down.

Slowly, Chance moved away a distance from Crandall. He stood easy with his hands at his sides. Parsons was ready and determined to build his reputation. The man's smile twisted his mouth. He was obviously trying to impress Hadley and Snow as well as the absent Rawlins. His eyes gleamed as he sneered with curled lip.

'Man wears two guns, he's just for show,' he growled.

'You pick the one you want.'

Parsons stood with feet apart. He had seen Chance make movements to his hat and bandanna with his right hand. Parsons hunched over a little as he spoke.

'Your left will do.'

Chance waited. There was going to be a gunfight here in the morning sun, right near the burned ranch house. Someone was going to die. Maybe both of them.

Hadley and Snow reined out of the line of fire. A sneering smile was set on Hadley's face. Snow, shorter and more sinister in nature, leaned on the pommel of his saddle to study the situation.

Crandall had his rifle leveled as warning against any interference. The air was still. No one moved.

Suddenly, Parsons went for his gun. Before he could aim, Chance had drawn with his left hand and fired. The bullet hit Parsons between the eyes. Stunned and dying, Parsons stared at him. Then he staggered backward, falling onto the hard ground with a thud.

Chance stood with the smoking Colt

in his hand. He looked at the other gunmen. Hadley smiled, shaking his head. There was a long, deafening silence. Chance hated what he had been forced to do. Anger simmered inside him.

At length, Hadley and Snow dismounted and picked up Parsons, throwing him over his saddle and tying him down. They remounted. Hadley sat straight in the saddle, reins in hand as he smiled coldly.

'Don't get brave, Darringer. Parsons was an easy kill.'

Snow grunted. 'Sure was. You ain't heard the last of us.'

The men turned their horses and rode off through the trees and out of sight. Chance drew a deep breath and holstered his weapon. Crandall slowly lowered his rifle.

'Glory be. Ain't never seen anything like it.'

'I was lucky.'

'You're faster'n a rattler.'

'Reckon I'm in for it now.'

'Well, you can change your mind, son.'

'I like it here. If you can cook.'

'Had you heard of them fellas?'

'Just Hadley. Figure he's plenty fast but square in a fight. It's Snow I wouldn't trust.'

Chance turned to his stallion and loosened the cinch. He wasn't too happy about killing a man in a gunfight. He'd fought with his hands, killing Apache and Comanche in many a confrontation. But this was the first time he'd faced a man with a gun to the end.

He didn't like it much. But Crandall's chattering helped him calm himself. He couldn't forget for a moment why he was here in this valley. Nothing must deter him.

★ ★ ★

While Chance was getting acquainted with the crusty old man, Susanna was at the Rawlins ranch, staring at the white satin she had bought for her gown. She felt trapped, with no way to escape the path she had taken. At times she was resigned, but she also had her moments of agony. She tried not to think of Chance, knowing he had a mission that didn't include thoughts of her.

That evening after an early supper, while Oscar was out at the corrals showing Becky her new pony, Susanna sat in the parlor. Maria, a Spanish woman with dark, careful eyes, served coffee. She walked softly from the room.

Susanna was alone with Silas Rawlins, and she was nervous. He came across as powerful and dangerous. Even when he tried to be fatherly, he looked hard and demanding.

'Susanna, all of this furniture was brought in from St. Louis. And I got a rosewood piano on its way. I recollect your ma wrote that you can play.'

'That was a long time ago.'

Just then, Becky came charging in.

She was wearing boy's britches and a jacket. Her blond hair bounced as she ran over to Susanna, sat with her on the couch, and grabbed her hand. Becky's eyes were round with excitement.

'You should see my pony! It's so pretty. Oscar's gonna fix the stirrups so I can ride tomorrow. Will you ride with me?'

'Of course.'

Becky had left the door open and a man stood in the entrance, darkness behind him. He was tall and slick with silver conchos on his hat band and fancy gun belt. Silas beckoned to him.

'Hadley, come in. Close the door. I want you to meet my son's fiancée, Susanna Ward, and her sister, Becky.'

Slowly, the gunman closed the door. Then he walked forward and paused a few feet from Susanna. He bowed gallantly. Becky giggled at his gesture.

But Hadley saw only Susanna. He moistened his lips. His eyes moved from Susanna's blue eyes and golden-brown hair to her shapely form. Her face burned, and she cringed under his gaze. Silas was impatient, however.

'What is it, Hadley? Did you buy the Crandall place?'

'No. I have to talk with you.'

'Susanna, would you and Becky excuse us? Maybe you'd like to turn in.'

Nodding, Susanna stood and led her sister down the hallway. Becky was sleepy and willingly entered her room, closing the door behind her. Susanna paused. She was out of the men's view, but she could hear them. Something drove her to listen.

Slowly, she moved back along the hallway and stood listening to the beating of her wild heart. It seemed forever before they spoke again. Hadley talked in a low voice.

'Burning Crandall's place didn't work. He was there this mornin', alive and kickin'. And he's got a new hand.'

'Who'd be fool enough?'

'He's a stranger. Chance Darringer.'

Silas grunted. 'So he's hired a fast gun.'

'And you're short one man.'

'What're you gettin' at?'

'Parsons took him on and drew first. But ole Parsons didn't even have a chance — Darringer drew and shot him right between the eyes. With his left hand.'

Grim, Silas bit on his pipe stem. 'Parsons was plenty fast.'

'So's Darringer. But I can take him. Any time you say.'

'No hurry. Just so they don't get them cattle to the Army. I don't want Crandall makin' his bank payment. And he's in pretty deep.'

'So what do you want me to do, Mr. Rawlins?'

'You and the boys hang low. Let Crandall rebuild. Then we'll burn 'im out again. It'll wear him down. But if they start movin' the cattle, hit 'em.'

'What about Darringer?'

'When the time comes, make it fair

and square. I don't want no law comin' around here. It's bad enough they sent someone when the sheriff was killed a year ago by some drifter. We were lucky it took him only a week to round up the killer. But this time, it would open up a whole bag of worms right here on the Rock in' R.'

Susanna drew a deep breath and started for her room, then stopped. She had heard the front door open and close. Oscar had arrived. Frightened that she might be seen, she started to move away, then stopped. No, she wanted to hear if Oscar was one of them.

Hadley told Oscar about Crandall and Chance.

'So Darringer turned back,' Oscar said with a snarl. 'I don't like a man who changes his mind. But I'll tell you one thing. He'd better stay away from Susanna or I'll plug him myself.'

'He took Parsons,' Hadley warned.

Oscar grimaced. 'That don't bother

me none. There's more than one way to kill a polecat.'

'Now look,' Silas interjected. 'We've been gettin' away with things because we go slow and easy. So you cool off, Oscar. You'll get everything you want in good time.'

Moving slowly backward, Susanna turned and hurried to her room, slipping inside and closing the door. She breathed more easily and slumped down on the bed.

Chance was back, and they wanted to kill him. She was frightened. Nothing was the way she had expected it to be. Oscar was obviously mixed up in some scheme of Silas's.

But Susanna couldn't go far as she had no money. Her sister had her first real home, a pony, and her own room. She'd have warmth, good food, protection, schooling. She wouldn't be dragged from mining camp to mining camp ever again. No more sleeping in tents or gullies for Becky, and she'd never be hungry again.

'Listen to me, Susanna,' her dying mother had begged as she held the tiny newborn in her arms. 'You've got to marry Oscar when you're old enough. And there'll be a home for Becky. Please, Susanna, it's all I ask. There's got to be an end to this.'

Susanna could still see the strange look on her father's face. Her mother's pleading had made it obvious that she knew their father could never take care of them when she was gone. He was a ne'er-do-well, a dreamer always seeking the end of the rainbow. Dragging them everywhere for nothing, he drank and gambled too.

Susanna's mother had died with Becky in her arms in a shack with a dirt floor on the edge of a mining town high in the foothills of the Sierra Nevada in California. No doctor had come to help, nor had anyone come to their aid. Rain had dribbled down through the roof, forcing them to move her bed twice. Sick with lung fever and the strain of childbirth, her mother had then closed her eyes forever.

And years later, when Grimey had come to fetch Susanna and Becky at the camp near the mine where her father had died, he had found them in another leaking cabin with a dirt floor, with only bread to eat.

Here they had everything her mother had wanted. Except Susanna was frightened. She prayed she would be rescued from this trap. And she prayed it would be Chance Darringer who saved her.

* * *

While Susanna was sitting with her face in her hands. Chance rode the hills with the old man. Crandall led the three horses that hadn't run away after the raid.

'I got me a shack up the creek. We can stay there. There's plenty of water, and it's well stocked.'

They made themselves at home. The shack was between two tree-spotted hills and set low by the creek — an easy target. Provisions were stored on shelves inside the single room. There was an iron stove, oil lamps, and two bunks. Tar paper covered the cracks in the walls, and the ceiling looked as if it would leak.

Crandall sat down wearily, a rifle across his knee. Chance threw his saddle and gear in the corner and sat on a bunk. He was plenty tired. The dog made itself comfortable on the rough wooden floor.

'Kinda crowded in here,' Chance said.

'You don't like it, you can draw your pay.'

Chance grinned. He liked the old man. When they had settled down, Chance told him about the Apache attack. He related how he came on the scene and saw Susanna trying to make a warrior drop Becky.

'There she was on his back, her arms locked around that big fella's neck and his ear in her teeth. I never seen anything like it.'

Crandall shook his head as he fixed their supper. They sat around the single table in rough-hewn chairs. Chance told about the canyon and Susanna's fall into the creek, and how brave she had been.

'But she bounced back. And she knew how to make us laugh.'

Crandall frowned. 'And she's gonna marry Oscar Rawlins?'

'That's the plan, I reckon.'

'Maybe we'll make her a widow before she's hitched.'

'You got somethin' in mind?'

Things are buildin' up around here, son. So far, the ranchers ain't organized. Everyone's too afraid. Ole Silas is pretty smart. He drives out one rancher at a time. The others kinda hide and hope that's the end of it. But he's after this whole valley. It's my turn, but I ain't movin' an inch.'

'If you had been home last night, you'd be as dead as that meat you're cookin'.'

'No, he wants me alive to sign over the deed, legal-like. Each ranch he got, he started by burnin' the place and killin' and scarin' off the hands. All by night riders. Then the owner would get fed up and sell out at Rawlins's price. But nobody can ever prove nothin'.'

'And there's no way to organize.'

'Not so far. Every rancher thinks he won't get hit if he lies low. They're fools — like I was. But I ain't scared, son. I got this game leg at Chickamauga, in the War Between the States. I seen enough killin', but I ain't gonna be scared off.'

'When are you plannin' your roundup?'

'Gotta get 'em out of the brush, then wait for 'em to fatten up a little. The calves look good. Grass is high now, and there's plenty of water in the creeks. And just maybe the United States marshal will show up before they try to stop us. Yeah, I wrote him three months ago.'

For a moment, Chance stared into space. The rancher noticed and fell silent. Finally, Chance spoke quietly.

'Listen, I've got somethin' on my mind. A girl I wanted to marry was murdered in Tombstone. I figure it was Oscar Rawlins, or Borcher or Lynch. Unless it was the man the Apache got. You know a fella named Hutch?'

'He wouldn't have done it. He was gentle as a kitten. Now, that Lynch is a bad one all right. But he never liked women much. Borcher, well, I would never turn my back on him. As for Oscar, I don't know. He's got a mean streak in him, all right. I reckon any of 'em coulda done it. What are you gonna do when you find this feller?'

Chance shrugged. 'I plan to turn him in. But when I find out who it is, I'm not sure I'll be able to do that. I might go crazy and kill him.'

'Every man's got that hidden nature, son, but good men rise above it.'

Chance wasn't so sure he could do that.

The two men talked into the night.

Before turning in, Chance told him about his family. Crandall said he'd not seen Kentucky since he was fourteen, when he ran away from home. He told of his Army days in the war.

That night Chance slept better than he had in weeks, but he dreamed of Polly. And sometimes, he dreamed of Susanna.

In the morning, Chance finished breakfast and downed his coffee before speaking. 'I'll start with you as soon as I get a look around Antler.'

'That's all right, son. I figure I'll rest up. Ain't so young anymore. Bein' outside all night at the ranch put a chill in my bones. We'll head out in a couple of days. Maybe by then they'll have worked their way down. Ain't no picnic up in that brush. It's tough on the horses.'

'Then I'll see you when I get back.'

'There ain't much in Antler. You'll have to spend the night. It's a full day there and another back. Rawlins owns half of it, including the bank.'

'Maybe I'll go out and have a look at his place.'

'That'd be a fool thing to do.'

Just then the dog stood up and growled. Crandall slid open the window shutter a crack, then made a face. 'Oh, no!'

'What is it?'

'Patience Smith. She's a widow who's got a small farm and orchard across the valley. Always bringin' me pies and cakes and shinin' up to me. How'd she find us, anyhow?'

With a grunt, Crandall went to the door and flung it open. Chance looked past him to see a small woman in her fifties. She was wearing a riding outfit and a man's hat over her gray hair. Her face was rosy, with dark, friendly eyes, and a genuine smile.

'So you're alive, you old field rat,' she said in a husky voice.

'How'd you find this place?'

'I tracked you. Why, I can trail a mountain lion on hard rock. You know I was married to an old Army scout.'

Crandall muttered under his breath as she entered. He watched as she helped herself to coffee and sat at the table. Then he introduced her to Chance. The annoyed rancher sat on the bunk as she reacted in surprise.

'So you got yourself a gunfighter? Maxie, you can't fight them all with one man.'

'Stop callin' me Maxie.'

She ignored his glare. 'Now then, Mr. Darringer, can you really use both those fancy guns? Or are they for show?'

'I can use both hands, all right.'

'Knew a fella like that once,' she said. 'He got all mixed up and shot himself in both feet.'

'Patience, why'd you come out here?' Crandall demanded. 'You know I'm a target. You ain't even packin' a gun.'

She reached in the pocket of her skirt and pulled out a small revolver. 'Smith and Wesson.'

'Well,' Crandall said, 'you probably

couldn't hit a bear if he was sittin' on your lap.'

'Any time you want a shootin' match — '

'Hey, listen,' Chance cut in, 'if you two want to stay here and argue, go ahead. I'm ridin' in to Antler, if you'll point me.'

'Ride due south,' Crandall said. 'About the time you spot a tabletop mountain, you'll see a wagon road. Head west. You'll get there by dark, I reckon. Patience, you ride out with him.'

'You afraid to be alone with me?' she asked.

Crandall grinned. 'You're darned tootin'.'

She laughed, pocketed her weapon, downed her coffee, then stood up. 'Come along, sonny. I'll get you pointed straight. Now, Maxie, you stay out of sight so you don't get hurt.'

Crandall glared at her as she left with Chance. The dog was left locked in the cabin with Crandall, who had agreed to watch over it. Having taken to the old man, it didn't try to get outside.

As Chance saddled his stallion. Patience mounted her gray mare.

'Maxie takes too many chances. Maybe you can keep him out of trouble till he can sell his cattle. He's got good crossbred beef, you know, better'n Rawlins's scraggly longhorns. They ain't as hardy but they got a lot of meat on 'em.'

Chance swung into the saddle. The buckskin shuddered with anticipation. They rode along the singing creek and into the clearing. She pointed him to the south and then went on her way.

It was late afternoon when Chance sighted the tabletop mountain and turned west along the beaten path. The wagon road was deeply rutted. The land was wide and rolling, with scattered dark pines and chunks of black lava that contrasted against the bright green of the grass. Soon, night fell. The stars were close and glistening in the black sky. The half-moon gave enough light to continue his ride.

As he neared Antler, he rode over a wooden bridge that crossed a busy creek. His stallion's hooves were loud on the creaky boards. He spotted the town in the distance. There were some twenty stores and a bank along a single street. The only lights were in the single saloon and some of the surrounding homes. At the far end was a livery with a good-size barn.

He reined up in front of the saloon and dismounted at the hitching rail beside three other horses. Inside, he found a simple room with tables and chairs. The barkeep was old with thinning hair and a fat face.

Two men sat at a corner table, drinking and playing cards. They looked like saddle tramps in their rough trail clothes. At the bar stood a tall man in a black leather coat, a Winchester under his arm. His Stetson was pushed back from his hard, lined face. Clear pale-blue eyes turned toward Chance.

Ignoring the man, Chance walked over to the bar and leaned on it. The barkeep approached, waiting.

'You got any cider? Or lemonade?'

He could hear the two men in the corner chuckling. Slowly, Chance turned to look at them. The bigger of the two leaned back in his chair, his puffy face cut with a grin.

'Hey, mister, if you can't handle a man's drink, why're you wearing them fancy guns?'

'So you can ask fool questions.'

The puffy-faced man turned grim. His partner, a skinner but tough-looking man, put his hands on the table as he spoke.

'Let's get him.'

'Yeah, we ain't had no fun in a long time. And I bet he's that gunfighter them Rawlins hands was tellin' us about. Why, if we take him, Rawlins will hire us for sure. And for top pay, I bet.'

The man in the black leather coat moved farther down the bar. Chance folded his arms, shaking his head.

'You fellas had best just ride on out. I don't want to hurt you.'

'Hurt us?' The puffy-faced man laughed.

The two men got to their feet slowly. The larger man spat on his hands and wiped them on his Levi's. The skinny one rubbed his grizzled face, ready to fight.

Chance stood with his arms folded, waiting. Suddenly, the puffy-faced man charged. Chance side-stepped, spun, and kicked the man in the rear as he grabbed him by the arms. With one continuous movement, Chance lifted the rushing man into the air and tossed him over the bar. Glasses shattered as the man crashed somewhere out of sight. His fall was so loud and heavy, the bar shook.

Chance turned as the skinny one rushed him, a knife in his hand. Chance ducked and caught him in the belly with his fist. The man gasped and doubled up, still holding the knife.

Chance slammed his head against the bar, then lifted him bodily. The man howled as Chance rolled him right over the counter. There was a crash, then silence. Nothing moved.

Chance reached for the cider he was finally offered.

'Patience Smith makes great cider,' the barkeep said nervously.

Then they heard clattering sounds. The two men were crawling behind the bar. As Chance sipped his drink, he heard a movement behind him. He spun as the puffy-faced man charged again.

Chance jumped forward, his knee contacting with the man's gut. The man gulped, eyes wide. Chance hit him on the jaw, resulting in a loud crack. The man fell backward and landed on his rear.

The attacker tried to get up, but was so stunned he was unable to rise. His skinny friend came from behind the bar, holding his belly. He helped the other man up. They glared at Chance with blazing hatred, then staggered out of the saloon.

'So much for that,' the bartender said. 'But you owe me for some broken glasses. About two bits, I'd say.'

Chance tossed the coins on the bar. Then he turned to look at the stranger in the black leather coat. The man was still holding the Winchester. His lined face was hard as nails but cut with a crooked smile and a white scar that crossed his chin. His clear blue eyes were unexpectedly friendly.

'Do I know you?' he said, his voice deep and quiet.

'Name's Chance Darringer.'

'Thought you had a familiar look. I know one of your kin — a lawman over in Colorado.'

'One of my half brothers.'

'You work hereabouts?'

'Just hired on with a fellow named Crandall.'

'Can I buy you another glass of that cider?'

Chance nodded. With their drinks,

they sat at a corner table, both managing to keep their backs to the wall. The stranger laid his Winchester on the table, aimed at the door.

'I'm a deputy U.S. marshal. Name's Drake.'

They shook hands. When Chance realized how intently the man was studying him, he felt uncomfortable, yet also curious.

'So where's your badge?' Chance asked.

'In my pocket, son. I hear there's a heap of trouble here. One of our deputies told me it didn't look too good last year as it was. I don't figure it's healthy to show my hand just yet.'

'But you told me. Why?'

'You're a stranger yourself. And you hired on with the man who wrote me for help.'

'I'll be needin' some of that.' Chance told him about Polly's murder, including the money-clip story. The lawman was intensely interested and promised to help find the killer.

'But you ain't got much to go on, son,' he said.

Then they discussed Crandall's problem at length. Chance told him about his experiences with the Rawlins party. He also couldn't help but describe Susanna and her courage. Then they downed their drinks and walked out into the moonlight.

The lawman was taken with the buckskin. 'Mighty fine animal. My horse is down at the livery. I was gonna bunk in the loft. You're welcome to join me.'

'Well, there sure ain't no hotel in this town.'

Chance loosened the reins from the hitching rail. Leading his stallion, he walked with Drake away from the lights of the saloon. It was searing cold, and stars glistened in the still, black sky. The buildings on either side of the street were dark.

The had gone only fifty feet when the bullets began to fly, whistling past their heads and thudding into the building behind them. One shot went through the brim of Chance's hat.

Both men dropped facedown on the boardwalk. Chance drew his right six-gun. The stallion danced nervously, then moved away as Chance released the reins.

The shooting had stopped momentarily.

Drake muttered under his breath, 'We got one second to get into that alley.'

4

Lying on their bellies on the rough boardwalk, the moon barely lighting the street, Chance and Drake knew they had to move — fast.

Both rolled over suddenly, jumped up, and dashed for the alley to their right. They leaped into the dark cover as bullets spat the ground behind them. Hitting the dirt hard, they recovered and backed to the wall of a building. Both were out of breath, hearts pounding.

'Comin' from that store across the way,' Drake said.

'No, they moved.'

'I'll get around 'em.'

'No, you stay here. I'm faster.'

Drake nodded grudgingly. He knelt with his Winchester aimed toward the store across the street. Chance moved out the back of the alley. He ran bent over, a six-gun in each hand, hammers pulled back and ready.

He cut behind the saloon, running until he was several buildings down the street. Then he slipped into an alley and looked carefully toward the store. He was certain he had seen movement from it in both directions.

Just the same, he was determined to get across. Drake opened rapid fire with his repeater, shattering the wood posts and corners around the store. Gunfire was returned. It sounded like an army.

Chance leaped up and ran as fast as he could across the street. Bullets cut at him, dirt flying around his boots. He made a dive for the alley across the way, grunting painfully as he landed on some old wooden crates.

The gunfire stopped. He heard running footsteps behind the building he was leaning against. He spun and charged down the alley in time to see two men mounting their horses. It was the saddle tramps from the saloon.

He sprang into the open, firing into the air with his right gun, then quickly recocking his weapon. The men turned and started firing back. He dropped to the dirt and fired at each man with both six-guns. Bullets spat in the dirt near his arm.

But it was over. Each man had been hit square in the chest. They fell crazily to the ground as their horses spun about. One man kept firing. Then there was a sudden moment of deathly silence. They lay crumpled against each other.

Chance rose to his knees, feeling the heat from his weapons. He heard running feet and turned as the law-man joined him. Drake came to an abrupt halt and stared at the scene. Then he went over and checked the two men. He turned, frowning.

'I'll be switched. You got 'em right off!'

'I fired in the air first. They wouldn't give up.'

Chance turned as they heard voices.

Four men who looked like merchants came through the alley with rifles. When they saw the dead, they stopped.

'What happened?' a fat man asked.

Drake explained without letting them know he was a lawman. They seemed to accept the story, although there was no one to dispute it. The barkeep also joined them and agreed the dead men had jumped Chance.

'Not much of a welcome for strangers,' the fat man said. 'My name's Bragg. I run the general store where the shootin' started. I appreciate your not breakin' my windows.'

The barkeep and the other merchants set about getting the bodies rolled into blankets and carted away, taking the horses with them. Bragg, Drake, and Chance went back into the street. The buckskin stallion came wandering toward them.

'You got any law around here?' Drake asked.

The fat man shook his head. 'No. First off, no one around here wants the job. At least no one who ain't in Rawlins's pay.'

'I'd recommend this young fellow here — Chance Darringer.'

'That a fact?' Bragg grunted, looking Chance over.

'I've got a job,' Chance said, uneasy.

Bragg was still interested. 'Let me talk to the others.'

Chance stood staring after him as the man waddled off. He took his stallion's trailing reins and turned to Drake, who started walking toward the livery. Chance caught up with him and protested, 'I already told you why I was here.'

The two men entered the dark livery. The moonlight falling through the cracks helped them find a stall for the stallion. Chance unsaddled and rubbed down his horse. Then he took his saddlebags and bedroll and followed Drake up the ladder.

As they slumped down on the crackly, itchy straw, Drake spread out his blankets. 'I've come a piece this day.'

'So if you're not tellin' folks you're a lawman, what are you planning to do?'

'I'll be ridin' out to talk to Crandall.'

'Then I'll be ridin' out to see Rawlins's place.'

'That ain't such a hot idea, except you're handy with your fists. And plenty good with both guns. How do you do that?'

'There's a fancy word for it, but I ain't either lefthanded or right. My brother Cole thinks we were supposed to be triplets instead of twins and I just ended up a mess.'

Chance reloaded his six-guns. He was getting mighty tired of fighting and killing everyone but the man he was after.

The two men made their beds and stretched out for the night. Chance told Drake how to find Crandall, then turned into his blankets. But he had trouble sleeping. Polly appeared in his dreams, along with Susanna and Oscar.

In the morning, the men had

breakfast at the saloon and parted company. Drake mounted his roan and cantered off toward Crandall's. Chance felt his day's growth of whiskers and decided he needed to clean up. For two bits, he had a hot bath and a shave behind the saloon. Then the barkeep gave him directions to the Rawlins's place.

'But I don't reckon you'll be welcome, Darringer,' the barkeep said. 'That's a mighty unfriendly bunch. They own half of the valley and are working to get the rest.'

'I just want a look.'

Chance went back to the livery for his stallion. He saddled and mounted, riding west. The rolling hills kept him from seeing much more than the mountain peaks to the south. Yellow flowers sprinkled the green grass. A redheaded woodpecker was working on a lone cottonwood by a creek.

By midafternoon, he spotted drifting longhorns on the far hills. A well-traveled path headed due west, probably to the ranch. He followed it awhile, then cut over into the northern hills and through a wooden gate in a wire fence.

On a rise, he reined up in the aspens and brush as he saw the ranch spread below. The house was big and rambling. It was a grand place for this part of the country. There were many corrals and outbuildings as well as a lot of men and horses. Some of the men looked heavily armed.

From about a quarter mile away he saw two other riders heading in from their day's work. It was Tolliver and Grimey, and both waving at him. Grimey rode over.

'Chance, you got no sense at all.'

'Just lookin' the place over. Looks like you got plenty of hands down there.'

'Hands? Well, you might say that. They can swing a rope all right. And we got near eight thousand head since Rawlins took over that Beeker ranch across the way. We all gotta put in time at the line shack and ridin' fence. But there's only about four of us mindin' the business full-time. Them fellas, they're too blamed good with their guns. And some of 'em just disappear now and then.'

'And ride all night?'

Grimey shrugged. 'I heard you was seen at Crandall's and you got Parsons. Him and Hadley and Snow, they never pretended to be here to herd cows. So you watch yourself.'

'You worried about me?'

'Maybe I am. You find out who killed your girl yet?'

'No, but I will. Reckon if I head northeast I'll circle around to Crandall's?'

'Eventually — and the sooner the better. You'll find a wire gate. And you'll cross over through Beeker's old place. When you see the brush country to the north, you'll know you're on the right trail. But, listen, you get to town on Saturday night and I'll buy you a drink.'

Chance reached over and shook the big man's hand. He watched him head for the ranch, then turned his buckskin toward the northern hills.

Out of view of the ranch, he saw two different riders stopped in the trees. One was a small girl on a pinto. The other had to be Susanna. Becky didn't see him and put her heels to her pony as if to race. She was on her way back to the ranch, full speed, laughing as she rode.

But Susanna didn't move. She had seen Chance's stallion.

She turned and rode back into the hills. Chance circled. Soon he could see her waiting in the trees. As he approached, she leaned forward on the pommel. She was astride a frisky sorrel mare. Wearing her riding skirt and a wool jacket, she looked prettier than he'd remembered. Her golden-brown hair was blowing in the wind. She smiled at him as he reined up.

'I'm glad to see you, Chance.'

'Looks like you've made yourself at home.'

Her smile faded. 'I have no choice.

And I hear you're working for Crandall. Chance, they plan to stop you from selling his cattle. I was eavesdropping.'

He hooked his right leg over the horn and pommel. 'You have to be careful about that.'

'I'm in no danger. But you are.'

He shrugged. The sun was warm, and there was no wind. It was pleasant sitting there looking at her. And strangely enough, he had no trouble talking to her. Her voice was soft, and sweet as cider.

'I heard Mr. Crandall's place was burned out,' she said.

'He's still got a shack up the creek. He's a grouchy old man, but I like him fine. How's Becky doing?'

'She's very happy. And the roof doesn't leak.'

'When's the wedding?'

'Oscar wants to be married next month.'

'What about you?'

'I told you, Chance. I have no choice.'

'I thought Grimey said your mother had a brother back East.'

She shook her head. 'Yes, but he was very sick. A letter she wrote from California before she died came back. It was marked 'Deceased.' We moved after that. We have no one else, except the Rawlinses. And they're not blood kin.'

Seeing her distress, he pushed his hat back from his damp brow. 'What's it like in California, anyhow?'

She brightened. 'Some of it looks like this. We saw big mountains and deep valleys. A lot of grass. Snow up high. But down in the southern part, there was a terrible desert we crossed to go into Arizona Territory. I thought we would all die from the heat. Becky was very sick. We had to stay at Yuma awhile. That's where the prison is.'

'Did you see the ocean?'

'Oh, yes. I was so excited, I didn't want to leave it. It was so beautiful. It roars like a lion and slides up the sand. And the fog lay out there on the horizon, then came rolling in all wet and cold.'

'I'd sure enough like to see it.'

She leaned forward slightly. 'I see you have some more bruises. Did you run into Lynch again?'

'No, just a couple of saddle tramps in the saloon lookin' to impress your uncle.'

They paused. Through the trees, they could see a distant rider heading their way from the direction of the ranch. Susanna paled, straightening. Chance put his boot back in the stirrup and pulled his hat down. It was late afternoon. The wind was rising, bringing a chill, and danger.

'It's Oscar,' she said. 'He'll be angry. You'd better go. I don't think he can see you in the trees.'

Chance didn't turn away. She became frantic.

'Chance, go now before he sees you. He's just coming to see why I didn't ride in with Becky.'

'I'm in no hurry.'

'If he sees us together, he'll have you killed.'

'I ain't worried.'

'You really don't care what happens to you, do you?'

He shrugged, realizing she was right. Since Tombstone, he had only one reason for living. But he couldn't bring himself to ride away from a man he disliked intensely. A man who could be his prey.

Chance sat patiently waiting for Oscar. Susanna became so frightened, she urged her mare into a lope out of the trees, heading downhill toward Oscar, who was approaching on his sorrel. Her silken hair flew about her shoulders.

She rode down to him and brought her mare into a walk as she neared. She was out of breath as she reined up beside him, trying to look cheerful. Her mare tossed its head. She smiled at Oscar, but he wasn't looking at her. She turned in the saddle to follow his gaze.

Chance came out of the trees on his stallion and rode down toward them at a steady walk. Her face turned hot with color. Oscar's piercing gray eyes were focused on the slowly approaching rider even as he spoke to Susanna in a hard, low voice.

'Where have you been?'

'I was just riding.'

'With Darringer?'

'He surprised me, that's all.'

Oscar looked just as he had when he beat the dead Apache repeatedly — brutal and crazed. She cringed and looked again toward Chance. If Oscar died tomorrow, she wouldn't cry. But if Chance so much as cut a finger, she would feel it. She didn't want anything to happen to him.

Riding up to them, Chance smiled. He showed no fear. Casually, he pulled his stallion to a halt and leaned on the pommel, looking with ease at the angry Oscar. He knew how to needle a man.

'Howdy,' he drawled.

'What are you doing here, Darringer? This is Rawlins land. And this is a Rawlins woman.'

'That a fact?'

'Ride off now, or I'll plug you.'

'Oscar, please,' Susanna said. 'You're making too much of this. We just ran into each other, that's all.'

'Get back to the house. Now.'

Anxious, she looked at Chance, who was still smiling. She started to rein off, then stopped, suddenly stubborn. Her chin went a little higher.

'No, I'll wait for you, Oscar.'

Furious, Oscar tried to read Chance's smile. He looked at the insistent Susanna. He was annoyed that she didn't obey. He swallowed his anger because he knew in time she would have to do as he said.

'All right, Susanna. Let's go back to the ranch. Just get off our property, Darringer.'

Chance just kept smiling. Oscar spun his sorrel about and rode away with Susanna. After a distance, she turned in the saddle to look back. Chance was still watching. Oscar reached over and grabbed her arm, turning her face forward.

Chance let his smile fade. He turned his mount back into the trees, convinced that Oscar would likely send his boys to hunt a Darringer. It was time to head for home anyhow. And he was mighty hungry.

It was nearly midnight when he got to Crandall's shack. The dog watched him as he entered. Over in the corner, on Chance's bunk, Drake was sound asleep. A lamp burned low on the table. The rancher was awake and gave him some coffee and a piece of the delicious apple pie that Patience had brought.

'You'd better marry that woman,' Chance said, savoring the pie bite by bite.

Crandall grunted and sat at the table with him. 'Drake ain't figured out a plan as yet. But at least he's here. Come morning he's gonna start a tour of the ranches and talk to people. He'll be gone a few days.'

'I rode out to the Rawlins place.'

'You see them two other hard cases?'

Chance shook his head. 'It's a big place, though — a lot of men and horses. Maybe twenty of 'em are more gunman than cowhand.'

'This valley is laid out like a checkerboard. They got the west half and two places on the east. Me, I'm on the north half with more land then they figure I got a right to.'

'So, what's next?'

'I rode out to have a look and saw a few head come down out of the brush. Cows and calves look good. Steers are fat and ornery. I figure soon as you get some sleep, we'll head out and try to get a count. You might get rich on your ten percent.'

'Patience said you had crossbreeds.'

'Had a big whiteface bull. It didn't make it a couple of winters ago, but it left me good beef and a young bull to carry on.'

★ ★ ★

While the men talked into the night, Susanna tossed and turned in her room. Her wrist still hurt from Oscar's grip. She was fearful he might hurt Chance. All the while, she kept telling herself that Chance could take care of himself.

At dawn, the Rawlins ranch was already busy. Men were at the corrals or on their way to the hills where the cattle grazed. Dark clouds obscured the sun whenever the wind blew.

In her room, Susanna dressed slowly in her riding clothes. She looked in the small mirror that hung over the lace-covered dresser. Her mother had wanted her to be a fine lady. Oscar wanted the same.

She turned to look at the roll of white satin she had bought in Tucson. If they were to be married next month, she would have to start making her dress.

And all the while, she kept thinking of Chance.

In the kitchen, she packed food for the picnic she and Becky had planned. She took rain slickers because she could see clouds moving in from the north. When she went outside and over to the corral, the cowhands were already in the saddle and heading out for the hills. Tolliver waved to her as he led them.

Becky was already saddling her pony in the near-empty corral. She was wearing her boy's clothes and looking happy. Her face was pink with excitement as Susanna handed her a slicker to tie behind her cantle.

'I could get on my pony and ride forever and never stop,' she bubbled.

'Will you stop for our picnic?'

'Sure. I got somethin' to tell you. But not till we're away from the ranch.'

Becky took off at a gallop in an easterly direction. Susanna shook her head, delighted her sister was so happy, but sad that it had to be here with Oscar. She saddled her sorrel mare and slid a Winchester into the scabbard. After tying down the slicker, she mounted and followed Becky at a distance. She liked watching her sister ride.

Becky didn't wait until they had their picnic. As they rested their horses on a ridge, she told her story.

'I heard that Mr. Hadley talkin' with Oscar outside my window last night. They were down below, but I could hear them plain.'

'And what did you hear?'

Becky made a face. 'I'm not real sure. But they know Mr. Crandall's been gettin' his herd down from the brush. They want to do something bad tonight — with a lot of men.'

'Did they say what?'

'No, but Oscar said he wanted Chance dead. Mr. Hadley said if it didn't work tonight, he'd see to it himself. That's all I heard. They went away.'

'Becky, you stay in the hills as long as you can. I have to warn Chance and Mr. Crandall. Take some of this meat and biscuits.'

'Oscar's gonna be mad.'

Susanna gave Becky some of the food and shoved the rest back in the sack hanging from her cantle. She knew the Crandall ranch was to the northeast, near the brush-covered hills. There would be a cabin by a creek. Nothing could stop her. Oscar would be furious, but maybe that's what she wanted.

Susanna buttoned her jacket at the collar. 'Oscar went to town this morning and will be late getting home. I'll try to beat him back. If anyone asks, you tell them you got tired, but I wanted to ride some more.'

'But what will you tell them when you get back?'

'That I got lost. I rode until it was dark and then got turned around. If it rains, I'll have found shelter for the night.'

'But Pa taught us how to read the stars, remember?'

'Oscar doesn't know that. Will you be all right out here?'

'Oh, sure. Me and Paint, we'll just ride slow.'

'Remember, you don't know anything about where I am.'

'I hope nothin' happens to Chance. I like him.'

'So do I, Becky.'

Susanna set her mare to a lope, heading northeast. She had all day to get there, but she knew she'd be lucky to be back before midnight. She saw some of the Rawlins's longhorns off to her left, but she didn't see any riders.

Soon it sprinkled off and on. The wind was cold and cutting. She pulled on the clumsy slicker and drew a scarf over her head.

Hours later she was at the Crandall fence. It was midafternoon before she found a wire gate. On the other side, she headed northwest.

Toward late afternoon, she spotted the brush-covered hills to the north, dark and dirty against the blue of the sky. There was another barbed-wire fence with a gate, which she entered.

Then she headed toward the brush country.

She began to realize what a fool she had been to come out here with no idea how to find Crandall, even though she knew the location of his ranch. But Chance had said there was a shack along a creek. Whispering prayers, she rode over a hill, then reined up short.

In the distance and to the east, she saw cattle coming down through the brush. A few calves stumbled along with the herd. Behind them was an old man and riding point was Chance on his stallion. Both wore leather chaps. They were far away, out of earshot. She drew the riffle from her scabbard.

Working the lever, she put a shell into the chamber, then aimed at the ground and fired. As the shot boomed and echoed, her horse shied.

Chance reined up, spinning about. He saw her and came riding at a lope. He soon pulled up in front of her weary mount, staring at her as she slid the rifle back in the scabbard. He looked hot and sweaty.

As she slowly dismounted, he swung down. She tossed her stirrup up over the horn and loosened the cinch. Her mare was damp with sweat. Chance walked over to her.

'Susanna, what are you doing here?'

'Oscar's sending some men after your cattle tonight. And he wants you dead.'

He frowned as he gazed at her. 'You'll be in trouble for this. Even if you ride nonstop, you'll be lucky to get home before midnight.'

'I'll be all right. What can you do?'

'I don't know. But I don't like your ridin' at night. Maybe I'll ride partway back with you.'

'No, if they're looking for me, you'd be in trouble.'

'I'm in trouble now.'

'But you'd be leaving Mr. Crandall alone. I'll be all right, Chance.'

She stood quiet a moment, her dark-blue eyes glistening in the fading light.

She wanted to ride with him, to use her Winchester for more than firing into the ground. Yet all she could do was wish. Sadly, she turned to tighten the cinch, dropping the stirrup.

She moved to put her boot in the stirrup. He brought his hand up to help her. Startled, she lost her balance and fell against him. He caught her in such a way that she was turned in his arms.

Brought up against him, she gazed through sudden tears at his wonderful face, with its strong nose and dark-brown eyes, the set square jaw and fine line of his mouth.

He wasn't aware of his movements. He saw the lovely face and the large eyes, the perfect lips and the little tip at the end of her nose. So like Polly. He felt the softness of her golden-brown hair as his fingers settled near her throat.

He bent his head. His lips found hers in a moment that lasted forever, until he drew away and caught his breath.

His face was burning. Tears trickled down her cheeks.

Slowly, his arms fell away. He watched as she turned and mounted her mare. She sat in the saddle, gazing down at him with a sad smile.

'Good-bye, Chance. God take care of you.'

He swallowed hard. 'Thanks for coming.'

She turned her horse and rode back toward the distant wire gate, leaving him shaken and still feeling her wondrous kiss. As he swung into the saddle, he felt as if his grieving heart suddenly had been shattered.

Could a man love two women at the same time? he wondered as he watched her ride out of sight.

★ ★ ★

Susanna was troubled as she urged her mare toward home.

Night had already fallen when she reached the wire gate. She crossed over

138

and rode into the trees. It was cold and the air was damp. She huddled in the saddle, hunched over and shivering. It sprinkled now and then. She could barely stay awake so she ate the picnic lunch in the saddle. The clouds had cleared enough for her to find the stars that pointed the way home.

At one point, she saw torches moving in the hills to the west. She didn't want them to find her. She wanted to ride in on her own, so she carefully avoided the distant riders.

Sometime later, with dawn still hours away, she became confused. The sky was black with clouds. She had no way to know whether she was still traveling in the right direction, and she was certain she was lost. Then she saw the lights of the ranch house.

Drawing a deep breath, she set her mare to a lope down the grassy hill, praying Oscar had stayed in town. At the corrals, she reined up and quickly dismounted. One of the cowhands was on guard and took her mare.

Spinning on one heel, she walked as fast as she could toward the house. Entering the parlor, she stopped cold. Silas was sitting in his leather chair. Oscar was standing by the hearth. Both men looked stern and angry.

Closing the door behind her, she smiled. 'I'm sorry I'm late. I was lost up there. But I had food with me.'

Walking casually to the fire to warm her hands, she ignored their steady gaze. She rubbed her back as if it was sore. She was trembling from exhaustion and cold. Her heart was drumming from fear of their anger.

'We've had men out all night lookin' for you,' Silas scolded. 'That was a fool thing to do.'

Oscar was furious. 'There'll be no more of it.'

She said good night and turned away as casually as she could. She walked down the hallway, hoping Oscar wouldn't follow.

'Susanna.'

She stopped cold, her heart skipping

a beat. She turned to see Oscar walking quickly toward her. Trying not to show her fear, she smiled at him. He grabbed her arm.

'Where did you go?'

'I told you, I got lost. Let go of my arm!'

'But you knew how to get back.'

'I was lucky. You're hurting me.'

He relaxed his grip. 'I'm sorry. I was worried. From now on, one of the men will ride with you.'

'But it's not necessary. I won't go that far anymore.'

'Just the same, a man will ride with you at all times.'

'If you wish.'

He gripped both arms now. Tense, she leaned back. He bent his head and kissed her hard, then he pulled her into his arms and hugged her tight. He kissed her cheek and became more gentle, his anger subsiding. He caressed her face and hair.

'Susanna, I don't want anything to happen to you. Don't you know I love you?' Slowly he released her.

She smiled and put her hand on the door latch. 'Good night, Oscar.'

Reluctantly he turned away. She slipped inside her room and locked the door, out of breath and trembling. She collapsed on her bed in tears.

★ ★ ★

'You'd better marry her pretty fast,' Silas told Oscar when he returned.

'Don't worry. I ain't lettin' her or that fortune get away from me.'

'From us.'

'Yeah, from us.'

'Don't you be forgettin', son, this was all my idea before you were old enough. It was me who did the plannin'. We're sharin', fifty-fifty.'

'Sure, Pa.'

Oscar sat down, wondering how he could keep Susanna's inheritance without sharing it with his greedy father. He figured he would find a way, because he would have no need for land and cattle when he had the money. Let his father have the valley. Oscar would have the world in his pocket, and a beautiful woman on his arm. He smiled to himself.

* * *

Meanwhile, Chance and Crandall were riding herd in the moonlight. They had already gathered over one hundred and fifty head, many with new calves. The cattle were fat and lazy. Most grazed near the creek that ran toward the shack, where they had planned to sleep that night. Now they would have to lie in wait.

'Maybe she was wrong,' Crandall said.

'They'll come from that hill to the west.'

'If they come shootin', we can't hold the cattle.'

'Then we gotta keep the herd away from the wire.'

They tied their horses in a gully east

of the creek. Then they took their rifles and blankets, finding comfortable spots in the rocks and brush between the cattle and the fence line. About forty feet apart, they sat quietly, listening to the night sounds. It was plenty cold. They took turns sleeping.

The black sky still threatened rain. Dampness hung in the air. *Maybe Susanna was wrong*, Chance thought. He was grim as he remembered Oscar's anger. He wasn't sure why she had taken such a chance to warn them.

He lay on his stomach, her face dancing before him.

Two hours before dawn, he was still gazing at the hill outlined against the western sky, his rifle ready. He didn't know how many there would be. Maybe they would ride right over him and Crandall. Maybe this would be their last night on earth.

Suddenly, he saw the first rider silhouetted against the sky.

5

Lying in the grass and dirt, protected by rocks, Chance lifted his Winchester grimly. Forty feet away, Crandall lay hidden in a gully. Some distance behind the two men, more than a hundred head of cattle milled near the creek. It was more than an hour before dawn and very cold. The low-hovering black clouds still threatened rain.

Suddenly, some twenty riders were riding like madmen down the hillside toward the wire fence. They fired their guns blindly but hit nothing. The first to reach the fence set his horse into a high jump.

Chance fired. The man stayed in the air as his horse cleared the fence. The rider fell like a rock and rolled in the grass. The other riders followed at a wild gallop. One of the horses didn't make the jump and screamed as it hit the wire, throwing its rider. Chance shot the man angrily as he got to his feet. The man keeled over.

Two men with ropes lassoed the posts and pulled four of them down. The others jumped their horses over the fallen wire. Chance and Crandall continued to fire with deadly aim, downing three more riders.

Now the raiders were on top of them. A fierce man with gleaming eyes bore down on Chance. He fired up in the man's gut. The attacker yelled and caught at his belly, doubling over in the saddle.

Six were down by Chance's fire. Crandall hit one. The others continued toward the cattle.

Chance stood up and fired with deadly accuracy. One more spun from the saddle. The others fired into the herd and then jerked their mounts around, riding straight toward the fallen fence. One looked like Borcher, another was wearing a bright-red vest.

Chance dropped back into the grass.

As the riders charged, he hit a small man with a beard. A bullet crashed through Chance's hat brim and creased his left shoulder. He felt the hot pain as he fired and missed. Nine were down. Eleven were heading back over the hill toward home. Not one of them had been wearing shiny conchos on his hatband or gun belt. These men were obviously expendable.

When he put his right hand on his left shoulder, Chance felt hot blood between his fingers. He got to his knees, worried about Crandall. But the old man was already checking the dead.

'We got nine of them devils,' Crandall said.

'We were lucky.'

'We had 'em cold. They never expected we'd be waitin'.'

'You figure they're Rawlins's men?'

'Ain't sure. But I seen a couple of 'em around town.'

Chance walked around looking at their faces as first light came from the east. 'They coulda been from Rawlins's ranch. I never saw 'em close up. Someone will recognize 'em.'

He went down to the creek and washed his shoulder. It hurt, but the wound was superficial. He bound his bandanna around his shoulder. Then he noticed that three head of cattle lay dead in the grass. He felt anger rising again.

At that moment, they heard the thunder of hooves. Coming up the creek from the direction of the cabin, further scattering the jittery cattle, was Drake. He reined up, rifle ready, his horse dancing as he surveyed the scene. Then he dismounted.

'I was at the cabin, wondering where you were. Then I heard shootin',' he said.

'We got nine of 'em,' Crandall told him. 'Susanna warned us. We was waitin'.'

Drake rolled one over with his boot. He looked at the others, shaking his head. 'Why'd she take a chance like that? Well, I don't know any of 'em. We'll take 'em to town.'

'By way of Rawlins's place,' Chance said.

Drake considered this. 'It might get the girl in trouble.'

'She's already in trouble,' Chance said, straightening. 'They'll figure we were warned.'

'It might throw 'em off if we ride their way,' Drake agreed. 'And I'll be wearin' my badge.'

'Let's move,' Chance urged them, worried about Susanna.

★ ★ ★

While Chance, Crandall, and Drake rounded up the stray horses and tied the bodies over the saddles, the eleven remaining raiders were hightailing it home.

By early afternoon, they straggled into the corrals, their horses winded and covered with sweat. The other hands were out riding herd or mending fence. They made it to the empty bunkhouse and collapsed on their beds.

Within the hour, Oscar Rawlins entered, closing the door behind him. He looked at their dirty, sweat-run faces. He wasn't one bit happy about what he saw.

'Where's the rest?' he demanded.

'They got nine of us,' one man reported.

'They was waitin' for us,' another said. 'We didn't even get to run the herd.'

'You get Darringer?' Oscar fumed.

'We didn't get nobody. They was dug in.'

'All right. Just keep your mouths shut about this. Get some sleep, then make yourselves scarce for a while.'

Oscar turned and went outside, slamming the door behind him. Nine men dead. He couldn't believe it. Maybe Crandall had just been smart and dug in, ready to wait for days for an attack.

Or they could have known it was

to be last night. Someone could have warned them. Was it Susanna?

Grim, he went back inside the house. Silas was sitting beside the hearth in his leather chair, reading one of those dime novels. Becky was on the rug, playing with a stick horse that Tolliver had carved for her. Susanna sat on the couch, doing needlepoint on white cloth framed in a wooden ring.

It was a serene picture of domestic tranquility, yet Oscar was raging inside, wondering if her night ride had been to warn Chance. He swallowed hard and sat near her on the couch. His voice was as tight as his insides.

'What are you sewing?' he asked.

'Something for our bedroom.'

Her smile and casual response threw him off guard. He leaned back on the couch and drew a deep breath, wondering why he had even thought she was capable of pulling off such a scheme. After all, she was just a woman.

'Did you get any sleep?' he asked.

'Oh, yes. And I had a hot bath.'

'Well, you remember. No more riding alone.'

She smiled again. She was afraid he might suspect where she had gone last night, so it was important to disarm him. And despite her longing for Chance, Susanna was determined to make the best of their relationship and future marriage. Within a few weeks, invitations would be sent out to wedding guests.

Oscar folded his arms. 'Why aren't you making your dress?'

'Oh, I am. In my room. You can't see it until the wedding. And I'm making a dress for Becky.'

As they talked, time passed rather pleasantly. Oscar calmed down, convinced that Darringer had just been prepared and that was all there was to it.

It was toward evening when Oscar, Silas, and Susanna walked onto the large porch to view the red and glowing sunset in the western sky. Soon it would be dark. Oscar put his arm around Susanna, holding her close. She tried to show affection by leaning her head on his shoulder. He liked it.

They drew apart as two riders approached. Two men were leading nine horses with bodies tied down across them.

Gripping the porch railing, Susanna's heart skipped several beats. Chance was in the lead. He looked handsome, sitting tall in the saddle. Yet his strong face was set in a frown.

Next to Chance was a stranger in a black leather coat. He had a hard, lined face. On his lapel he sported a shining badge. Oscar and his furious father ignored Susanna as they walked down from the porch into the cold twilight.

Drake reined up, gazing down at them. 'You know these men?'

'I don't know *you*,' Silas growled.

'Drake. I'm a deputy United States marshal. Mr. Crandall's ranch was attacked last night by twenty riders. Two steers and one cow were shot dead. These nine men were killed in the raid.'

Oscar came forward and looked at some of the faces. 'Well, yeah, they may have worked for us. But they sure weren't paid to do any night ridin'.'

Drake was grim. 'Their belongings are in this saddlebag.' He tossed it down to Oscar. 'None of them are wanted men. Go ahead and bury 'em.'

Chance sat tight in the saddle, watching Susanna. She was so beautiful, he couldn't bear to think of her being anywhere near Oscar Rawlins. His skin crawled at the thought of any woman being in danger or harmed.

As if reading Chance's mind, Oscar went back to the porch and put his arm around her. 'You're welcome to come in for supper.'

Drake leaned on the pommel. 'Maybe we should have a talk at that.'

'What about you, Darringer?' Oscar taunted.

Chance didn't want to leave Drake alone in the lion's den. He shrugged and nodded. Some men came from the bunkhouse to take care of the horses and the dead riders. One was Grimey, who put a hand on Chance's shoulder. Drake stayed to listen. The others had already gone in the house.

'Glad to see you're still alive, Chance.'

'Them other fellas come ridin' in sometime today?'

Grimey looked around to be sure the three of them were alone. 'They were here, all right. Slept some, I figure. I don't know where they are now.'

'I think I'd recognize two of 'em. One looked like Borcher. The other was small and wiry, wearing a fancy red vest.'

'That one sounds like Pitts. He'd as soon gut you as look at you. Mighty fancy with a knife, so watch out. But he and Borcher, they ain't here right now. Neither is Lynch.'

'Lynch wasn't on the raid. Snow and Hadley around?'

'No. I heard Oscar tell Hadley this

mornin' to get into town because he was expectin' a letter from some fancy lawyer back East. Maybe Snow went with him. Where's that wolf-dog of yours?'

'Back at Crandall's. He's taken to the old man.'

'Bite you yet?' Grimey asked, grinning.

Chance shook his head and they gripped hands. Then Chance followed Drake into the big ranch house. He was surprised by the lavish furnishings and the great hearth. The dining area was in another room. Maria served them roast beef, potatoes, and apple pie.

'Don't know what we'd do without Patience Smith,' Silas said. 'She's the only farmer I ever liked.'

Seated next to Drake on one side of the table. Chance looked directly at Oscar. Susanna was to the man's left. Silas was at the head of the table. Becky sat to Chance's left. She was chattering happily about her pony.

Trying to be casual, Susanna talked about California. But Oscar wasn't listening — he was too busy glaring at Chance.

Silas turned to Drake. 'How long you gonna be around here?'

'I don't know,' the lawman said. 'I don't like the way things look.'

Silas grunted. 'There wasn't any trouble till you came.'

Looking distressed, Susanna again talked of California. 'In the spring, the hills are green and covered with wildflowers. Corn grows tall. They cut hay more than once. It's a farmer's paradise in the valley.'

'If I was there,' Oscar said, 'I'd be up in the mines.'

'Those are terrible places.' She shuddered. 'Men are always fighting. There's no real law. They want three dollars for a single egg. And there are hardly any schools. My mother taught me my letters, and I taught Becky hers.'

Drake sipped his coffee and looked directly at Oscar. 'When you and your men were in Tombstone, the night before you left, a woman was killed. One of your Rockin' R money clips was found near her body.'

'Anybody coulda had that clip,' Oscar snapped.

'I'll want to talk to the men who were with you in Tombstone,' Drake continued. 'And some who might have hit Crandall's last night. Like maybe a man named Borcher. And a fella named Pitts. Maybe I ought to bunk in your barn.'

'We have rooms here,' Susanna said quickly.

Oscar frowned but nodded. 'Sure, you and Darringer can have one down the end of the hall.'

They sat around the hearth and talked awhile. Susanna sensed they wanted her to leave, but she was afraid. As long as she stayed, maybe there wouldn't be trouble. The men did talk more carefully with her watching them. The conversation turned to politics.

'And Fremont's plannin' to dig this canal,' Silas said.

Drake nodded. 'But a few years ago, it was suggested by the *Overland Monthly* that fresh water from the rivers could be diverted to the desert. Then you wouldn't need a canal comin' in from the gulf.'

'It's all foolhardiness,' Silas said. 'Ain't nothin' ever gonna grow down in them wastelands. And if it did, it'd just bring in more farmers. And we ain't got room for 'em.'

★ ★ ★

They all retired at the same time. In their room, Drake and Chance turned up the lamp, and Chance stretched out on one of the beds and said, 'Maybe Borcher and Pitts will take off now that Oscar knows we got a fix on 'em.'

'Don't worry. We'll get 'em.'

'Sure, just you and me against eleven of 'em. And maybe Hadley and Snow. And the Rawlinses. Good odds.'

'Ain't nothin' new to me. Lawmen don't have much help out here. But I figure I should deputize you. If things get rough and I get killed, it'll keep you from hangin'.'

Drake pulled a badge out of his saddlebags, a circled star that shone in the lamplight. Chance stared at it. He was hesitant, but he knew Drake was right. And it just might come in handy for finding and holding Polly's killer, if he didn't end up strangling the man first.

The lawman swore him in, then pinned the badge on his shirt. Chance stared down at it, shaking his head. He lay back on the bed and rested his hat over his face. He never had expected to wear a badge. Now he didn't expect to stay alive.

In the morning, the two men joined the Rawlinses for a hearty breakfast. Susanna wore her riding clothes, and Becky babbled happily about how they were going on a picnic. Oscar brooded, while Silas just sat and puffed on his smelly pipe, his gaze wandering back and forth between Chance and Drake.

The gleaming badge on Chance's shirt had caught everyone's attention, but no one mentioned it.

'Your men ride back last night?' Drake asked.

Silas nodded. 'They came in, all right. If you think they're the ones you want, go ahead and take 'em, if you can.'

Oscar leaned back in his chair. 'Maybe twenty men didn't hit ole Crandall's. Maybe them nine was just ridin' through nice and easy like, and Crandall and Darringer here just shot 'em down. The rest of the boys was probably in town havin' a drink. I figure Hadley and Snow even spent the night there.'

Susanna was frightened at the dangerous conversation and tried to make small talk. She was ignored.

'You parade 'em out,' Chance said. 'I'll recognize at least one of 'em.'

Oscar smiled. 'Go ahead to the bunkhouse. Have a look.'

'Parade 'em out,' Drake said.

Oscar turned to Susanna. 'You and your sister stay in the house till this is over.'

Susanna sat frozen in her chair, staring after them. When the men had gone outside into the morning sun, she ran to a front window, pulling aside the heavy drapes. Becky pushed close.

'What are they gonna do, Susanna?'

'I don't know.'

She left Becky at the window, went over to the large gun case, and took out a new Winchester repeater. It was already loaded, and she worked a shell into the chamber, then went back to the window. She didn't know what she was going to do.

Outside, the four men walked toward the bunkhouse. The old cook was over by the well, filling a bucket. He stayed there when he saw the badges.

Oscar went up to the bunkhouse and kicked open the door.

'You men come out here, pronto.'

It was a while before ten sleepy gun hands came outside. One was missing, and there was no sign of Snow or Hadley. Lynch wasn't among them. The more serious cowhands had already gone to work. It was obvious these men had another calling besides cattle.

The gunmen tucked in their shirts and pulled on their hats. Each one wore his side arm. Not one had on a red vest. They stood around, waiting. Their eyes showed defiance.

One was a stout man with a large nose and black mustache. It was Borcher. The moonlight raid came clear in Chance's memory.

'Borcher's one of 'em,' Chance said, pointing. 'And the others look plenty familiar. But one of 'em is missing. A small man with a fancy red vest. Pitts.'

Drake nodded to Borcher. 'You. Where were you the night before last?'

'Me and these fellas were in town that night and all day yesterday. We got home late, that's all.'

'But you know what we're talkin'

about,' Drake said.

Borcher shrugged. 'No, I don't.'

'Well, Mr. Borcher, you're under arrest. Drop your gun belt, slow and easy.'

The man stiffened, his hand near his gun. Then he looked at Oscar, who shook his head. Just the same, the man didn't unbuckle his belt. His mouth twisted under his mustache. His eyes narrowed to slits.

'I ain't goin' nowhere, Marshal. I didn't do nothin'.'

The other gunmen were coming to life. They formed a half circle on each side of Borcher. Oscar and Silas stepped aside. Chance moved to Drake's side.

Tension hung in the air. If wild shooting started, a lot of men were going to die.

Chance kept his eye on the other men. He could hear his heart driving itself wild. He figured Drake could outgun Borcher, but he didn't want anything to happen to the lawman. He was going to need him when he found Polly's killer.

Suddenly, Borcher drew. Chance pulled his right six-gun and fired at the same time. Borcher was hit in the chest. He gasped in pain, then he dropped to his knees and fell on his face, dead. Drake had drawn, but Chance had been faster.

Both Chance and Drake kept their six-guns leveled. The other gunmen stood ready. No one moved. Then the men began to shuffle and hook their thumbs in their gun belts. The fight was over.

'Another one to bury,' Drake said, slowly holstering his gun. 'Chance, you recognize any of the rest?'

'I ain't real sure.'

'Then we'll be ridin'.'

Drake turned and walked toward the corral and their horses. Chance stood watching the others. He allowed Drake to saddle up both mounts as the gunmen slowly turned and went back into the bunkhouse, with only three remaining outside.

Drake led out the horses. Chance watched Silas and Oscar with their smug looks. But he breathed easier. A possible disaster had been avoided.

The two lawmen mounted and rode out toward the aspens and cottonwoods that lined the ridge near the ranch. Silas went into the bunkhouse, as did the cook. Oscar and three gun hands stood watching the men riding away. He was smiling, yet apprehension danced on his face.

As they neared the trees, Chance saw the sun glisten on the leaves of the aspens. He felt an inner warning but saw nothing. There were several cottonwoods and some brush. It was a cluster that could conceal death.

Suddenly, a rifle shot rang out. The lawmen drew their weapons. There was a rustle in a cottonwood over to the left. A little man in a red vest with a repeating rifle in one hand and a six-gun in the other was trying to hold on to a limb. He dropped the revolver. He dangled from the branch, wild-eyed. Blood was on his chest. Then he fell heavily to the ground.

Astonished, Chance and Drake turned in their saddles. Susanna was on the porch, lowering her rifle, while two of the men at the bunkhouse were slowly holstering their six-guns. Another rested a rifle on his shoulder. If Susanna hadn't fired, Drake and Chance would have been caught in a cross fire. The two of them would have been buried and forgotten plenty fast.

Drake rode around the dead man. 'This must be Pitts. It was a fool thing for him to do, thinkin' he could get both of us. I reckon Oscar put him up to it. An easy sacrifice. Oughta be some money in his pocket, all right.'

'I figure his friends were about to back him up.'

'Well, we can't prove it.'

Drake dismounted, recovering five ten-dollar gold pieces. He straightened, tossed them on the dead man, and got back in the saddle, shaking his head.

In his arrogance, the man hadn't even stashed a horse for a getaway.

Chance couldn't take his eyes from Susanna. She stood tall and beautiful and defiant. He was proud of her spunk, sorry for her predicament. He tensed as he saw Oscar stride toward her.

Chance spun his stallion about and rode up just as Oscar reached the steps. Becky came running outside. Susanna stood unmoving as Becky grabbed her hand.

'Well, thanks,' Chance said, leaning on the horn as he smiled at Susanna.

Oscar was speechless, standing there with his hand on his holster looking for all the world like a stunned madman.

Shaken from what she had done, Susanna handed the rifle to Oscar, who was still unable to speak. For a moment, she stared at Chance, her lips trembling into a smile. Then she turned and went back inside the house, with Becky following.

Oscar found his voice. 'Well, I sure

didn't know Pitts was in the trees. What was he doin' out there, anyhow?'

'Maybe you put him up to it,' Drake said as he rode up. 'Maybe you figured it was a way to bury us both, once and for all.'

'Pitts was just a hired hand. How'd I know what he was gonna do? We needed extra hands for the roundup. He was a fool.'

'Trying to take both of us?' Drake asked.

'He was a little crazy, that Pitts,' Oscar insisted.

Silas was walking over from the bunkhouse, but Drake was too angry to wait. He spun his horse about and headed east. Chance followed, but he kept looking over his shoulder until they were past the trees and over the hill.

Then Drake reined up. 'I'm goin' into town to see what I can learn. You'd better get back to Crandall's.'

'Watch out for Hadley and Snow.'

'I know 'em both,' Drake said.

'Hadley's a face-on fighter. Snow will get you any way he can. So you watch out yourself. They'll be paid plenty for the job.'

'See if you can find out why Rawlins is getting a letter from some fancy lawyer. Do you want this badge back?'

'No, put it in your pocket. It might keep you alive.'

* * *

Back at the Rawlins ranch, Susanna was in her room with the door locked. She was still shaken. Trying to kill an Apache in battle had been one thing. Deliberately shooting a man out of a tree to save Chance had been different. She felt sick to her stomach.

Soon there was a pounding on her door. She straightened, suddenly pale and trembling all over. Her knees buckled. She put her hand on the bedpost.

'Who is it?'

'Oscar. I want to talk with you.'

'I'll be out in a few minutes.'

He seemed to accept that and went away. Her heart beating wildly, she pulled herself together. Her mother's wishes were farther away in her mind. Life was changing too fast.

She went into the hallway and over to the hearth where Oscar waited alone. She was afraid but refused to show it. She smiled and warmed her hands. He stood so close, she could almost feel his fury.

'Susanna, why did you do that?'

'Do what, Oscar?'

'Shoot that man out of the tree.'

'He was going to kill the marshal.'

'Or Darringer. Look at me when I talk to you.'

Slowly, she turned, gazing up at him innocently. He gripped her arm in his strong fingers. She tried to appear calm and unafraid.

'How did you know Pitts was there?'

'I didn't. I saw the sun on his rifle.'

'Where did you learn to shoot like

that?' he demanded.

'From my father.'

'Susanna, you're going to be my wife. I want you to be a fine lady, not a mining-camp trollop like your ma.'

Staring at him, hot with anger, she drew back. Then she slapped his face so hard it numbed her hand and nearly shattered her arm.

Furious, Oscar hit her back with his free hand. The blow struck her on the jaw and knocked her head back. She nearly fainted. He had to catch her and hold her steady. She swayed, barely able to stand.

As he helped her to the couch, he glanced toward the safe where her legacy awaited her twenty-first birthday. Her uncle had become wealthy with his ships. An empire awaited her — and Oscar. He'd better not throw it away so easily.

'Susanna, I'm sorry, honey. Are you all right?'

She shook her head, still stunned. He kissed her hands and her face. He had his arm around her and squeezed her frantically.

'Susanna, it was a trigger reaction. I'm sorry. Please forgive me. You surprised me. I just lost my head. Honey, I would never hurt you. Please say you forgive me.'

She gazed up at him, unable to answer.

'Remember, honey, it's what your pa wanted. We even sent him money. And you know your ma started writin' us when we was both youngsters. She had it in her mind to — Say, we still have her letters. Hold on.'

He got up and went to the safe, spinning the combination, then moving the handle. He took out the little bundle of letters inside and brought them to her.

'Here, honey. Every one of them talks about you. And the last one's about Becky. There's some from your pa. Read them. You'll feel better.'

She gazed at him blankly, knowing he wanted her to feel guilty if she didn't follow her mother's dying wish. Taking the letters in her trembling hands, she nodded. Then she struggled to her feet and walked away.

He stood watching her go down the hallway to her room. Smiling, knowing the letters would bring her in line, he went back and locked the safe.

In her room, Susanna lay on the bed and read her mother's letters with tears in her eyes. The most tragic were when she was expecting Becky. All voiced the hope that her daughter and Silas's son, Oscar, would marry when they were old enough. Her mother was driven by fear of further poverty.

It was the three letters from her father that startled Susanna. The first letter was written over five years ago from California. She read his words over and over.

. . . I'm enclosing a lawyer's letter that my wife got after she died. It's from her brother's lawyer. Something about a will that left a little money

for Susanna when she turns twenty-one. But I can't wait. Maybe you could find out for me how much it is and lend me some money against it. I need a grubstake real soon . . .

She stared at the letter until tears blurred her vision. She wiped her eyes and looked at the second letter, written when she was sixteen, from a Nevada mining camp.

. . . I thought I'd never hear from you, Silas. You sure took a long time. But I sure appreciate the five hundred dollars you sent. So let me get it straight. There's about two thousand dollars that Susanna will receive when she's twenty-one. If you send me another five hundred, then I'll send her up there so she can marry Oscar. I sure need a grubstake. I'm enclosing a picture so you can see she's a comely young woman . . .

Sniffing back her tears, she opened the third and last letter, written from Tombstone just before he died in the mining accident last fall. As she read it, she felt her body going cold from the inside out.

. . . I got the second five hundred, but I need more. I know I'm gonna make a strike any day now. Send me another five hundred. That's only fifteen hundred all together. You'll get another five hundred you can keep. She'll be married to Oscar when she gets it, anyhow.

I'm enclosing a new picture of Susanna. You send me the money, and I'll send her to you . . .

Susanna lay back on the bed, pain shooting through her. Oscar had purposely let her read her father's letters. Was it to hurt her? She could understand why he gave her her mother's letters — to make her feel guilty. But to have her read that her father had spent her small inheritance was brutal.

★ ★ ★

While Susanna wept, Oscar was out at the corrals, talking with his father. 'That crazy Pitts. I gave him money to ambush 'em — but not here on the ranch, for cryin' out loud. I told him to get them on the trail to town. And to take Borcher with him.'

Silas grunted. 'You knew he was crazy.'

'Can you believe Susanna shootin' him from the tree?'

'You're gettin' a good woman there. I coulda used a wife like that when I settled here. Your ma, bless her soul, was too weak for this country.'

'Everything would be fine if Darringer wasn't around. And that marshal.'

'Then put Hadley on 'em.'

'No, I think I'll try Snow. That way, I know it'll be done, because Snow ain't too particular how he kills a man.

And there'd be no witnesses.'

'All right, go ahead. But don't pay him more than five hundred for either one. And don't be in a hurry. It's gotta look like an accident so they can't tie it to us. I'm sick and tired of their interference with my plans.'

'Our plans, Pa. And maybe it wouldn't hurt to let it get around that Darringer's worth five hundred. We gotta cover our bets,' Oscar added. He could hardly wait for Snow to return from town. He would be rid of Darringer once and for all. And he wouldn't mind seeing the last of the marshal, either.

★ ★ ★

Days later at the Crandall ranch, Chance and the old man watched the cattle graze peacefully in the hills. The animals were fat and sassy. Drake had stopped by once, saying he had learned nothing in town and was on his way to visit some of the other ranches.

Chance was still in turmoil. He didn't have any proof against Oscar or his men, and he was tired of waiting. Yet he had stumbled to a halt in his search. He felt like beating the truth out of Oscar. But he couldn't help but wonder if Borcher or Lynch or even the man lost in the Apache raid could have been the killer. Worse, maybe it was some stranger back in Tombstone, walking around undetected, never to be caught.

Some days later, Chance started out for town to get supplies. He and Crandall were planning on moving the herd soon, without warning, so they were stocking up a little at a time and living on the cabin's provisions.

At the same time, Drake was in Bragg's store, buying a piece of candy. He had a sweet tooth and hated to admit it.

'Say, Marshal,' Bragg said, 'there's a man who just got here from Tombstone, lookin' for Darringer. Feller named Beale. I told him you were here, and he wants to talk to you. He's over at the saloon.'

Drake thanked him and crossed to the other side of the street, enjoying the warm sun. Then he went inside, where the barkeep was chatting with a stranger.

'It's quiet now,' the barkeep said. 'But you oughta see some nights in here. Poker fills this place up. Especially on Saturday and payday.'

The man wore a leather coat over his stocky frame. He had a white scar on his face. But he looked friendly enough.

'Marshal, I'm glad to see you,' he said. 'The name's Beale.'

They went to a corner where they could talk out of earshot. Beale looked weary as he downed his drink.

'Me and my men came out of our way to stop here. We're headin' for Santa Fe. But I had to find Darringer.'

'Is it about the murder in Tombstone?'

'Yeah. He came to the house after Miss Polly was killed. Her ma had found her, and couldn't talk. Darringer left because he figured it was someone from the Rockin' R.'

'So why are you here.?'

'It was two days before we could get Polly's mother to talk sense. It seems that when we came back from my ranch and I dropped her off at the house, she went inside and found Polly in the sewin' room. Polly had a pair of scissors tight in her right hand. They were covered with blood right up to the handles. She musta stabbed her killer pretty deep, probably in the back. All her ma could think to do was wash the scissors. That's why she was sittin' there with 'em when I got back.'

'Even if we found a man with a scar, a knife makes the same — '

'No, Marshal,' he interrupted. 'You see, these scissors had long, skinny blades. A knife blade's usually a lot wider. Now, Miss Polly was right-handed, so you oughta look behind some feller's left shoulder. I came here to tell Darringer about it.'

'I'll pass it on. And for now, maybe I'll take a ride out to the Rawlins's place and start pullin' off shirts.'

Beale seemed to relax. He had done what he came for and was ready to leave for Santa Fe. Drake thanked him and rode out that morning.

★ ★ ★

It was late afternoon when Chance rode into Antler. He didn't know about Beale, and Drake was gone. Chance was driving the wagon and a team of black geldings. His buckskin was tied behind, just in case he wanted to do some riding. The dog rode in the back of the wagon.

The street was empty except for two small boys playing near the livery. An old man was asleep on the bench outside the saloon. Chance fastened the reins and jumped down.

Bragg was behind the counter when Chance walked into the store. He was going through his books and looked perturbed. When he saw Chance he brightened, because Chance had paid cash on his last visit. Chewing on a cigar, Bragg leaned on the counter and grinned as he read Chance's list.

'You and old Crandall sure get hungry. And it sure helps. Rawlins lent me money. Now he's breathin' down my neck.'

'You seen the marshal?'

'Yeah, this mornin'. Some feller from Tombstone was here lookin' for you, but he talked to the marshal instead. Don't know what he wanted. Then Drake rode out right after. So did the stranger.'

Hope raged within Chance, and he paced around while Bragg gathered the supplies.

'My wagon's outside. I'll be back,' he said. But as he walked onto the boardwalk, he realized Bragg wouldn't go anywhere near the wagon with the dog in it.

He went over and put his hand on a back wheel. 'Listen, Pardner. You gotta come with me.'

The dog snarled but stood up. To Chance's surprise, it jumped out and followed him down the street toward the saloon. Three horses were tied at the rail. Inside, he recognized three of the gunmen from the Rawlins ranch, all of whom could well have been on the raid.

One was tall and skinny with a scar on his chin. Another was chunky and mean looking. The third was cross-eyed, his mouth twisted in a snarl.

'Look what just crawled in,' the third man said.

Chance ignored him and went over to the bar. The dog lay down near him. The barkeep didn't wait to be asked. He brought him some of Patience's apple cider.

'You seen the marshal?' Chance asked.

'Yeah, he was talkin' to some feller from Tombstone, but they left. I don't know what it was about.'

'And look at that mangy dog,' the

cross-eyed man continued.

'His brother, all right,' the skinny one said.

Chance ignored them and turned his back. He knew he was taking a risk, but he figured Rawlins wouldn't let them do anything foolish, at least not in the open. The rancher didn't want trouble with Drake. Besides, Chance was in no mood for a fight. He was so upset, he might kill these men with his bare hands.

'Hey, Darringer. Did you know you're worth five hundred dollars?' one asked.

Chance stiffened. A price on his head already? Rawlins hadn't wasted any time.

'Maybe he can't fight like a man,' the other said. 'Anyone can fire a gun. Wonder how he is with a knife.'

'Yeah. He had to have a woman save his neck.'

Chance downed his cider, his back still to them. He heard a chair scrape the floor. One of them spat across the room and missed the spittoon. The ugly tobacco juice splattered on Chance's boot. The dog growled. Chance spun around as the chunky man came at him with a knife.

The dog jumped up and sprang, clamping its big jaws around the man's arm. Yelling in pain, the man kicked at the dog. Chance slammed his fist in the man's face, knocking him silly. As the unconscious fellow hit the floor, the dog let go.

Angry, the other two jumped to their feet. The cross-eyed man pulled a long knife and moved menacingly. The other circled. Chance kept his gaze on the knife-holder's face, his hands ready.

'You and them guns,' the cross-eyed one said. 'Let's see if you can fight like a man.'

Again, the dog sprang up and grabbed the knife arm, chomping down as the man yelled. Chance shoved his right fist in the man's gut, doubling him over. Then he hit him on the jaw, sending him sprawling over backward and slamming back on the table as the dog let go. The man hit the floor, rolled over, and lay still.

The skinny one was blazing mad. He pulled a knife. but kept it close to his belt.

'Can't you fight without that mangy cur?' he taunted.

Chance turned to the snarling dog. 'Stay.'

To his surprise, the animal backed away and sat down.

The killer came at him with blazing eyes and a wild knife, slashing as Chance jumped from side to side. 'I'm gonna cut you good, Darringer. And then I'm gonna collect that five hundred!'

6

As the skinny man with the knife moved around him, Chance danced a little. He saw the man's skill, the size of the blade, and the spot he was in.

He moved around so he was away from the bar and near the tables. The man lunged. Chance grabbed a chair and lifted it. The knife slammed into the wood and right through the seat, almost cutting Chance's chest.

Tossing the chair and imbedded knife aside, Chance charged the man. They grappled, fell to the floor, and rolled. Pounding each other, they gasped for breath and strength. The man was strong as a bull.

The man pushed Chance away, then caught him in the jaw with his boot. Stunned, Chance could barely see the man leap suddenly from the top of the bar. He was struck hard. They fell to the floor, fighting for control, hitting hard until neither had much strength left.

Finally, Chance landed a good blow on the man's jaw, and he keeled over, unconscious. Badly shaken, Chance sat on the floor, barely able to see. He was a wreck.

He got to his feet, backed away, stepped into the spittoon and lost his balance as his boot and the brass container sailed off the floor. He staggered backward, grabbing at the bar, but he missed. As he hit the floor, his head struck the front of the bar. Dazed, he slid down to lie on his back staring at the ceiling. He tried to rise and couldn't. He was just too tired.

The big black dog started licking his face. Startled, he tried to push the lapping tongue away. The dog then licked his hand. Chance rose on his elbow and put his fingers in the tight fur, scratching the big neck. Eerie yellow eyes fixed on him.

Chance sat up slowly. The dog drew back. Its tail didn't wag, but then it was part wolf.

Getting to his feet and leaning on the bar, Chance gratefully accepted some cider from the grinning barkeep, who had been hidden behind the bar.

'You ought to come to town more often, mister. It livens things up around here.'

'Well, they come at me, you know.'

'If there's a price on your head, you'd better watch your back.'

Chance turned to see some faces at the entrance, behind the swinging door. One of the men was Bragg, the others were just curiosity seekers. Seeing the three unconscious gunmen on the floor, they wandered off.

After downing his cider, Chance paid the barkeep and tossed in an extra dollar for cleanup. Then he went for his supplies and paid Bragg, who again suggested the idea of Chance wearing a badge in Antler. Chance declined and loaded up the wagon. The dog jumped in beside the boxes.

He wondered if Drake had headed for the Rawlins place, so he circled the long way in that direction. Maybe he'd see Drake on the trail somewhere. He could always swing east when it got dark. It was cold, and he pulled his hat down tight.

Hours later, as night fell, he saw the trail that cut over toward the Rocking R. Reluctantly, he headed the team toward home. Maybe Drake was at Crandall's, waiting for him.

Moonlight came and went with the clouds. Once he thought he saw a rider ahead of him in the trees. He told himself he was just seeing ghosts.

But as he drove by a creek through a nest of cottonwoods, he began to sense trouble. He peered about in the darkness. The dog rose to its feet in the back of the wagon, snarling.

Suddenly, a bullet whistled by his chin, then another shot singed his left hand. He slapped the reins on the team and sent them into a trot, then a fast gallop. More shots rang out, missing him. One struck the wagon.

Over the hill he drove, fast and wild. Soon he felt he was in the clear. He reined up the team and jumped down, then freed his stallion. He mounted it and rode like the wind the way they had come. The dog raced behind.

As he reached the cottonwoods, Chance slowed. The dog charged on ahead, sniffing the night air, then trotted through the trees. Suddenly, the animal snarled.

Over on the next rise, a man leaped down from the rocks on to the back of a horse. Chance set his mount to a gallop as the man tried to get away. In the moonlight he caught a glimpse of shiny conchos on a hat-band.

His stallion closed the gap easily. As he came up next to the rider, he saw a six-gun aim at him and fire. He ducked and rose out of his saddle, then leaped, landing on the man. They crashed to the ground in a heap, sprawling and fighting for the man's gun.

'Blast you!' the man snarled.

It was Snow, the sinister gunman. Chance pounded his face and peeled the gun from his hand. Snow grabbed Chance by the neck and jerked. He beat at Chance with his other hand. They rolled into thorny brush. Snow yelped.

Chance broke free, but Snow grabbed his leg as he got up. They went down, rolling around in the grass. Snow slammed a fist in Chance's middle. Gasping, Chance hit him on the jaw, hard. Both men scrambled to their feet.

Snow charged like a wild man. Chance put his boot in the man's gut and shoved him away. Furious, Snow fell over backward but got to his feet. Chance stood up quickly, and drew his six-gun.

'Go ahead and shoot, Darringer.'

'You're under arrest.'

'What?'

With his left hand, Chance reached into his pocket for the badge. Clumsily, he pinned it on his shirt. Snow stared.

'You tried to ambush me, Snow. You musta seen my wagon in town. You rode on ahead, knowing I was comin' this way. I'm gonna lock you up.'

Snow laughed. 'We got no jail.'

'We'll find one.'

'You got no witnesses.'

'I got you. Now keep your hands up.'

They stood looking at each other, the moonlight shining on the gun in Chance's hand. He signaled the man to start walking. Snow protested.

'I'll lead the horses. Go on back to my wagon,' Chance said. 'It ain't far. I got some rope there.'

Snow walked ahead with his hands in the air. It was dark, cold, and damp. Snow was as mad as a wet cat and snarling to himself. He wasn't looking forward to being hog-tied. Chance walked behind with Snow's horse and kept his six-gun aimed at him.

Suddenly, Snow reached into his coat and pulled a knife. He spun and threw as Chance fired. The bullet hit Snow right in the heart. Snow gasped, eyes wild, and died before he hit the ground.

Chance felt a searing pain and looked down to see the knife embedded in his leg. He reached down with a quivering left hand and jerked the blade free. The knife had sailed downward, leaving a gash six inches long.

He tossed the knife aside, pulled out his bandanna, and wrapped it around his thigh, but the blood came through. Somehow he mounted his stallion and rode to the wagon, where he dismounted and tied the horse behind the bed. The dog jumped up inside with the supplies.

Chance barely made it up to the wagon seat, the pain in his leg was so bad. The closest help was the Rawlins ranch, just over the hills to his left. The town was hours behind him, and Crandall's cabin was even farther ahead.

He turned the wagon toward the

ranch. Blood was running down his leg and into his boot. He pressed one hand on the wound, but he had to let go to handle the reins. He was getting dizzy as he set the team into a fast trot. Over the hills they went and down the slope toward the ranch.

It was after ten at night, but lamps burned in the windows of the bunkhouse and the main building. He drove right up to the ranch house and reined the team up short. They reared and snorted loudly.

Climbing down, his leg on fire, he staggered toward the porch. The front door opened. It was Silas, holding a lamp.

'Who's out there?' he demanded.

Chance lurched up the steps.

'What do you want, Darringer?' Silas snarled.

'One of your men knifed me.'

Suddenly, Susanna was at the door. She was wearing a green dress with lace. Frantic, she came forward and slid her arm around his waist. He put his arm around her shoulders and hobbled alongside her. She guided him over to the fireplace. He could barely stand.

Maria was setting a tray of coffee on the small table. She straightened as Susanna called to her.

'Hot water, Maria. Lots of it. And a knife. And alcohol.'

Chance slid sideways onto the couch. Maria brought the knife and alcohol. She laid a folded sheet on the rug, under Chance's boot, then went back for water.

Susanna knelt and pulled off his boot as he winced in pain. She cut away at his Levi's. The denim was tough, but she persisted until the wound was bared. She ignored the blood stains on her gown. Chance sat watching her busy hands through a haze as he fought to remain conscious.

It was then he saw the pale bruise on her chin. He felt hot anger rising within him. He knew Oscar was responsible.

Silas closed the door and stomped back over to the fireside, glaring at

Chance. 'What do you mean, one of my men knifed you?'

'That fellow named Snow tried to ambush me in the trees a couple of miles east of here, but he's a lousy night shot. Then he pulled a knife. I had to kill him.'

'You killed Snow?'

Chance nodded. 'And three of your gun hands tried to knife me in the saloon. You'll find 'em still unconscious on the floor, most likely.'

'You don't kill easy, I take it.'

'Maybe you ain't offerin' enough.'

'You're loco.'

'Word is, you put five hundred on my head.'

'Ain't so.'

Susanna paused and looked up from Chance's leg. She stared at him and Silas. Her color was gone, making the bruise stand out.

Maria brought a pail of water with rags and soap, setting it on the floor by Susanna, who washed the deep, ugly slash carefully, almost burning it with the water and harsh suds.

'You've had practice,' he said, wincing.

'My father was in a lot of fights.'

At Susanna's direction, Maria went to Susanna's room and brought needles and silk thread.

'I have to stitch it up,' she said.

The front door opened and Oscar entered. Through his dazed vision, Chance saw a pleasured sneer on Oscar's face.

Determined to ignore the pain, Chance looked at Oscar as calmly as he could. He tried to appear nonchalant, even as Susanna started stitching.

'What happened?' Oscar asked as he sat down in a chair near the coffee table.

'Snow tried to kill him,' Silas said. 'I wonder why.'

Oscar shrugged. 'Yeah.'

'Three of your bounty hunters jumped me in the saloon,' Chance said. 'You can go pick 'em up off the floor.'

Oscar folded his arms and leaned

back. 'You're a pretty tough fellow, I take it.'

'That's a fact,' Chance said.

He looked down to see tears in Susanna's eyes as she finished tending his wound. After she bandaged it, she put his foot on a stool. He managed to smile and thank her as she stood up.

Oscar frowned. 'You should have let Maria do that. Ain't fittin' for the lady of the house.'

Susanna just smiled and went to wash her hands. Then she sat on the couch near Chance, pouring him some coffee and handing him the cup. Chance took it and sipped the hot liquid with pleasure. Then he looked at Oscar and Silas.

'Well, nine of your gun hands are dead. Three are beaten up in town. Snow and Parsons are done for. That leaves eight hangin' around here, plus Hadley and Lynch.'

'You're wearin' out your welcome,' Silas told him.

'He has to spend the night,' Susanna said.

Chance shrugged. 'I'll be all right. I'm drivin' the wagon.'

'You have to stay the night,' she insisted. 'You have to keep that leg elevated.'

'I'll get Grimey to drive him home,' Oscar said, rising.

Susanna wasn't too happy about the decision, but she nodded.

As Oscar went outside, Silas lit his pipe and looked at Chance with obvious dislike. 'Maybe you ought to be thinkin' about leaving for Montana.'

'He has a job,' Susanna reminded him.

'That was his first mistake.'

Chance turned to look at Susanna. He wanted to talk with her in private and find out if Oscar had hit her because she had warned him and Crandall. But he was hurting right now, and his head was still spinning.

Oscar came back inside. 'Grimey's

201

saddling up. You can get movin',
Darringer.'

Chance tried to stand. Immediately,
Susanna was there to steady him with
her arm. Oscar looked furious but said
nothing.

She helped Chance to the door and
onto the porch. He grabbed the post
with his free hand. She felt good
against him, soft and feminine. It made
him think of Polly.

She released him as they waited for
Grimey. Oscar came to stand near her.
His face was dark with anger.

'Go back inside, Susanna.'

'I want to see that he gets on the
wagon all right.'

'Grimey will take care of him.'

'I want to be sure.'

'You're gonna have to get over that
stubborn streak. It ain't fittin'.'

The night was cold with clouds
moving across the starry sky. They saw
Grimey riding over from the corrals.
He dismounted and tied his mount to
the rear of the wagon alongside the

stallion. Then he came forward.

'Can you help Chance into the back of the wagon?' she asked.

'Sure thing.'

Grimey walked over to the steps, took Chance's right arm, bent over, and tossed Chance bodily over his shoulder. Chance grunted as his middle hit the man's giant muscles.

Grimey turned around and walked to the wagon. He rolled Chance onto the sacks and boxes next to the dog. The pain of the disturbed stitches was excruciating. Chance muttered under his breath and then tried to get comfortable. Grimey climbed onto the seat and took up the reins, turning the wagon toward the hills.

★ ★ ★

Oscar ushered Susanna back inside and ordered her to her room. Then he turned to his father.

'I'm gettin' tired of this mess, Pa. Looks like it's gonna take the whole crew to get Darringer. And even then I ain't so sure. He's some kind of devil.'

'He's just flesh and blood. We'll get him. And say, that marshal was here lookin' for you. He was talkin' to the boys about that killin' in Tombstone.'

'I don't know nothin' about that. But I'm thinkin' it's time I just took Susanna and them papers away from here. There's got to be a better place than this.'

'No better cow country.'

'Maybe I've had my fill of cattle.'

'You listen to me, Oscar. Those papers and that woman are not leavin' this valley, even if I have to marry her myself. And don't be laughin' like that. I'm more of a man right now than you'll ever be!'

★ ★ ★

While the Rawlins men argued in the house, the wagon continued up the grade in the moonlight. Chance

204

grimaced in pain with every bounce of the wagon bed. The dog crawled over and laid its head on his belly. He rubbed its neck.

'You comfortable?' Grimey asked over his shoulder.

'Yeah. You seen Drake today?'

'He came by yesterday about that woman who was killed in Tombstone when we were there.'

'What did he want to know?'

'Who was with us in Tombstone, and if anyone left our camp that last night. But I didn't know — I sleep pretty good. Borcher was on guard part of the night. Then Lynch was on guard toward mornin'. But I reckon either one coulda left and not one of us would have known it. That's all I could tell him.'

Grimey cracked the reins to move the horses up the hill a little faster. He continued, 'Then the marshal came back today. Seems he saw this feller Beale from Tombstone. This feller said before the woman died, she'd likely stabbed the killer in the back with her scissors.'

Chance felt a ray of hope. 'So Drake's lookin' for scars.'

'Somethin' like that. Oscar wasn't on the ranch. I didn't know where Lynch was either, but me and Tolliver pulled up our shirts and showed him we was clean. But you know what? Ole Tolliver's got six scars from bullet wounds all over him. He was hit at Shiloh, but he came back alive.'

Chance was thoughtful. 'When you were camped at Tombstone, did any of the men act funny in the morning? Like they were wounded?'

'Drake asked that too, but I don't recollect.'

Chance lay back, rubbing the sleeping dog's neck. His thigh was painful and throbbing, but he didn't mind — not now when there was hope. If the killer were Oscar or Lynch, he might have a scar on his back from a stab wound. He remembered Polly's mother holding the long, thin scissors as if she were petting them. She must have washed them off and thought only of the dress Polly had told Chance she was making.

Grimly, he realized that if the man with the scar was not found, the trail could come to a dead end. His thoughts were lost as he fell into semiconsciousness. The hours in the rocking wagon gave him a chance to rest from the loss of blood.

He was well rested when they reached Crandall's place. He directed Grimey to a gate and across the hills to the cabin by the singing creek. It was nearly dawn.

Pulling as close as he could to the trees blocking the cabin path, Grimey rolled the wagon to a halt. He climbed down and reached up for Chance. The dog snapped at his fingers.

'Fool dog!'

Chance grinned as he sat up sleepily, pushing the dog aside. He allowed Grimey to carry him to the door. The big man kicked at it with his boot.

After a moment, the door creaked

open. Crandall squinted in the early light, then let them inside. He turned up the lamp as Grimey deposited Chance on the nearest bunk like a child. The dog lay next to him.

'You'd better make this feller a crutch,' Grimey said.

'What happened?' Crandall asked.

As Chance filled him in, Grimey unloaded the wagon, carrying heavy sacks under each arm as if they were sticks. Soon the supplies were all stacked inside the cabin, taking up more room than the men themselves.

Grimey went out to take care of the team and the stallion. Then he came back inside and shared hot coffee with them. Chance managed to sit up and elevate his leg. He insisted he would be all right as soon as he rested, but his head was still foggy.

'I'm figurin' it's about time to start roundin' up them steers for Fort Wingate,' Crandall said. 'As soon as the calves are marked and branded, that is. There's plenty of grass on the trail. I could use another hand, Grimey. Especially since Chance is cut up.'

'I gotta keep an eye on Miss Susanna and little Becky.'

'I'll be in the saddle tomorrow,' Chance insisted. 'But I gotta see Drake first. Has he been out here?'

Crandall shook his head.

★ ★ ★

As the men talked in the shack by the creek, Drake awoke in the loft of the livery in town. He'd been told about the fight in the saloon between Chance and three of Rawlins's men. He knew there was a price on Chance's head.

Drake had expected to find Oscar in town, but he'd missed him. He'd found no sign of Lynch. One of the two men could be a killer. Now he'd have to ride back to the Rawlins ranch.

He left the livery for a hearty breakfast at the saloon, then spent most of the day visiting merchants and asking questions, particularly about the night riding. In the late afternoon, he went over to Bragg's store. While he was buying bullets, he noticed a jewelry case. There were two Rocking R money clips in with the beads and baubles.

'Mighty pretty,' Drake said.

'Do a lot of tradin' after the Saturday-night poker games,' Bragg said. 'Them money clips are in and out of here all the time.'

'You seen Oscar Rawlins this morning?' Drake asked, then frowned as he saw Bragg's surprise. He turned to look at Oscar, who was standing in the doorway, his hands on his Winchester. He was outlined against the sunlight.

'The men said you were lookin' for me.'

'They tell you why?'

'Sure did. And I figure it's pretty funny.'

'Then peel off your shirt.'

'Marshal, maybe you forget, but you're talking to a Rawlins. We don't jump for nobody. We own half this country around here. And no tin badge is gonna come in here and shove us around.'

The two men stood firm in their tracks. Bragg found a safer spot behind his counter. A woman started to enter, paused, and left quickly. A thin man with a cigar came wandering in, oblivious to the others, and looked at the boots hanging from the ceiling near the far wall.

Drake's gaze was serious, his mouth tight.

'Well, it don't matter,' Oscar said, suddenly smiling. 'Sure, I'll let you have a look, but not here. Maybe in the back room where it's private. Then I'll be glad to buy you a drink.'

Drake took a few steps backward toward the store-room, his hand reaching for the door latch. Oscar just grinned and walked past him toward the opened door, Winchester still in both hands. Yet there was an eerie gleam in Oscar's eyes and his mouth turned sinister.

Suddenly, Oscar spun and slammed the butt of the rifle in Drake's face, hitting him low on the forehead. It made a terrible cracking sound. Drake staggered backward, grabbing at the air as he dropped to the floor. He tried to rise, then twisted, fell, and sprawled against the boxes. He lay lifeless in front of Oscar, who laughed.

'That'll teach him to roust a Rawlins.'

Bragg ran over to the hurt man, turning him over. 'Oscar, you killed him.'

Oscar was surprised. He stood a moment assessing the situation. He was so used to being the only law in the valley, he had almost forgotten that Drake had any power.

'It was an accident. You both saw it.'

Frightened, the thin man was no danger to Oscar. But Bragg would not be intimidated. He was furious, his fat face pink. His voice was quavering with his anger.

'Your pa can take my store, Oscar, but I'm testifyin' you killed this man in cold blood.'

'You don't scare me none, Bragg. Besides, ain't no law gonna come after a Rawlins.'

'Maybe Darringer will have something to say about that.'

Irritated, Oscar waved his rifle at them. 'Get back, both of you. And nobody from this two-bit town better show their faces at the ranch, neither.'

He moved a few steps at a time, backing toward the door, where he paused, glancing out at the empty street. He waved his rifle menacingly at the two men. There was a wild look in his eyes. Even Bragg backed off as he stared at him.

Then Oscar slammed the door closed and ran for his horse. He was breathing hard, but he wasn't one bit sorry.

Bragg looked out the window. 'Let him go. They'll get him, sooner or later. No posse can get onto Rawlins's spread. We'd all be killed for sure.'

'What about Darringer?'

'Ride out to Crandall's and find him.'

'This is bad,' the thin man said.

'You'd better find Doc and send him over.'

'He ain't dead?'

Bragg knelt by the marshal, his hand on his chest. 'I ain't sure, but I think he's breathin'. Hurry up.'

The thin man turned on his heel and rushed outside.

Meanwhile, Oscar rode furiously back to the ranch. His mind was churning. His father would protect him only if it didn't cost him the valley. Silas was just as ruthless and self-serving as his son.

Oscar didn't want the ranch. All he really needed was Susanna and the papers showing that she would soon inherit a shipping fortune. He was tired of herding cattle. He had better ideas for the kind of life he wanted — the life of a gentleman in some big city, with Susanna on his arm.

He reached the ranch after midnight. The place was dark and there was no sign of life. At the corral, he saddled two fresh horses and threw a pack saddle on a mule. At the house, he silently gathered supplies and loaded the mule.

Then he went back inside and opened the safe, taking out a handful of greenbacks and the legal papers, shoving them inside his shirt. He was going to be a rich man. Nobody was going to stop him from marrying Susanna.

He wrote a short note to his father. Then he drew his six-gun and headed up the hallway toward Susanna's room.

7

It was morning when Chance awakened. He was wearing new Levi's. Crandall poured him some hot coffee, while Patience, who had come over with apple pie, fussed over him. Chance liked the attention — it made him think of Texas and his own mother's gentle hands. But he was in a hurry.

'I gotta find Drake.'

'You ain't movin',' Patience said firmly.

Trying to rise, Chance felt nauseated. His leg was on fire. But all he could think of was Drake. He wanted to ride with him, to pull the shirts off Oscar and Lynch. Even if the scars weren't visible, one of them might crack under pressure.

A vision of Polly under that blanket flashed before his eyes — the woman he had loved, covered with blood, brutalized by some animal. Chance felt that same knot in his middle. He had to do something.

But he was too sick, and fell unconscious despite himself. He awakened at midday with blankets heaped on him. His fever had broken. His left thigh was still sore and throbbing where Susanna had sewn it. He remembered her gentle hands and the bruise on her chin. His face burned with his wrath. Then he heard the dog growling.

A thin man with a raspy voice came in as Crandall opened the door. Patience poured him some coffee. The man was out of breath and looked ghostly. Excited and frightened, he blabbered out what had happened to Drake.

'But Drake ain't dead,' the stranger said. 'He was in some kinda coma when I left. Doc says he may never come to.'

'I'd better see him.' Chance struggled to stand up.

'Go ahead,' Crandall agreed uneasily. 'Use the wagon.'

'My horse is faster.'

Patience insisted on riding to town with Chance and the thin man. She had had some nurse's training, and felt she could help. Using a crutch that Crandall had made from a tree limb. Chance hobbled onto the porch. The buckskin was saddled for him. Chance mounted from the right side. The pain was almost unbearable.

It was dark when they reached Antler. The only lights in town were at the doctor's. The man was actually just a medic who had learned his trade in the war, but he did have some understanding of head injuries.

Bragg sat on a chair near the bed as they entered. He hurriedly told them what had happened. Patience checked Drake, who lay still and unmoving, as if asleep. Chance stared down at him, his hands turning into fists.

The doctor shook his head. 'He may wake up, or he may die just like that.

Or he could wake up blind.'

'That doesn't tell us much,' Patience said, annoyed. 'I'll stick around and see if I can help.'

Chance was so angry he had to go outside to cool off. He threw the crutch against the wall of the building. His fury overcame the searing pain as he hobbled into the street.

Bragg followed. It was cold and dark as they walked to where the stallion was tied. Chance pulled the badge from his pocket and pinned it back on his shirt under his leather coat.

'I'm headin' for the Rawlins ranch.'

'Let's talk first,' Bragg said. 'I'll buy you some supper. And you'll be better off if you wait till you've had some sleep. You may need some supplies too.'

Chance had to agree and limped reluctantly toward the saloon as Bragg gave him further details of the attempted murder.

'Wasn't like Drake to be that careless,' Chance said.

'Reckon he thought that with witnesses around Oscar wouldn't do anything. Besides, Oscar was laughing about it. Nobody would have thought he had anything to hide.'

'Oscar must be carrying a lot of guilt to make him do a fool thing like that.'

Bragg shook his head. 'Not necessarily. I've known that man a long time. He's got a mean streak. I seen him beat a man near to death. And once he kicked a dog all over town.'

Chance grimaced. There was no easy answer. He still didn't know who Polly's killer was. As he thought of her, he realized he had kept his grief buried far too long. He felt cold clean through.

They reached the saloon and went inside. It was empty. The barkeep ordered food for them, and they sat in the corner at a table. They moistened their lips when they received their steak and beans.

'So what are your plans, Darringer?'

'I gotta find Oscar. And I want to see Lynch.'

'But there's a price on your head. And you know they have about twenty gunmen on hire out there.'

'Eleven. And Lynch.'

'That's right. I heard you got some of 'em. But Hadley's back in town. He's got himself a big reputation. I saw him up at the livery about an hour ago. Maybe he's tucked himself in.'

'No such luck.'

They both looked up just as Hadley wandered in. The tall man's hard face was dark from the sun. His hooked nose had a bead of sweat on it. The conchos on his hatband and gun belt gleamed in the lamplight.

Leaning on the bar, he turned to look at Chance and Bragg. He sneered. 'Buy you fellas a drink?'

Bragg shrugged and stood up. 'Not me. Thanks.'

The barkeep, a little nervous now, brought Chance more of the steaming coffee. Chance let his coat fall aside to reveal the badge on his shirt.

Bragg walked out the swinging doors, then sidled up to a window to peer inside. The barkeep got behind the bar, ready to duck.

The sinister gunman kept smiling at Chance, who continued to eat his steak with relish.

'Darringer, I don't like your face.'

Chance ignored him. The steak was good and tender. The beans were hot. The coffee was steaming. He was in no mood for any kind of challenge. He wanted to finish his meal, maybe get a few hours of sleep, then head out to Rawlins's place and try to arrest Oscar.

Hadley was annoyed that Chance was ignoring him. He moved away from the bar to the center of the room, his hands loose at his sides. His side arm rested in a cutaway holster.

'Darringer, I hear you been botherin' Miss Susanna. We don't take kindly to that around here.'

Chance cut another chunk of steak.

Hadley walked up to the table, reached down, and grabbed the plate. He threw it aside. The food slammed against the wall. Chance sat looking at it.

The bartender dived behind the bar, and Bragg moved back from the window. Hadley backed away from the table.

Chance lifted his coffee cup and took a long sip. He looked up at Hadley. The man was ready and waiting to kill for money. The trouble was, there was a good chance Hadley was faster than Chance.

Hadley made his living by hiring out his gun. He had killed a lot of men in fair fights because he was faster. He was deadly because he didn't care if he lived or died.

Chance took another sip of coffee. A lot had changed in his life since he came to this valley on the vengeance trail. And he had many a good reason to fight. Polly, the dirty tricks played on Crandall, the cruel blow that put Drake into a coma. Oscar's mistreatment of Susanna.

And this man who stood in the way of Chance's putting Oscar in custody. Yes, Chance was afraid — afraid Hadley might kill him and prevent him from doing what he had to do.

'Darringer, I'm figurin' your blood is pure yellow.'

Chance stood up slowly. His leg throbbed. He held the coffee cup in his right hand, watching Hadley. He sipped the hot brew. He wasn't steady on his feet.

'Remember, Darringer, I seen you draw. I'm faster. So if you want, you can turn tail.'

'All this for five hundred dollars?'

The gunman sneered, backing away a few steps. 'Nobody has to pay me. I've been waitin' for you.'

'Well, go shoot yourself. I got somethin' better to do.'

As Chance set his cup down and hobbled toward the door, Hadley spoke quickly, his voice a little higher. 'Well, then, let me tell you my plans. When Oscar's not lookin', I'm gonna have my fun with Susanna. She likes me, all right.'

Chance felt sweat on his back. He wanted to shove his fist in the man's ugly mouth. Very slowly, he turned and looked at the sinister Hadley. Chance's coat was confining. He pushed it away from both guns. Hadley snickered. The air was still, stifling, dry.

Slowly, Chance moved to put his back to the wall as he waited. Hadley's fingers were twitching. The man's eyes narrowed suddenly. It was now.

Hadley drew fast. Chance drew his right gun at the same time. Both men fired. Shots rang out. Smoke dribbled from the ends of their guns.

Blood dribbled from Hadley's shirt, near his heart. He stood calm and serene. Then his knees buckled, and he dropped to the floor. He stared at Chance, who stood in front of him. He couldn't believe he had missed. Chance moved forward.

'Who paid you, Hadley?'

But the gunman was dead. Chance backed away, sweat on his brow. He told himself it was necessary. And he thought of the men who Hadley had killed, some of them innocent victims.

Then he heard running feet outside on the boardwalk. He turned around, six-gun in hand.

Becky came charging through the swinging doors, her face pink, her eyes red from crying. She was out of breath, gasping for air. When she saw Chance, she cried out his name.

He holstered his gun and reached to catch her as she fell. He helped her to a chair. She was near collapse and frantic. Bragg followed her inside.

'What's wrong?' Chance asked, pulling up a chair.

'Last night, real late — ' Becky managed to gasp. 'I heard noises in the hallway, but I wasn't awake at first. I finally got up and saw Susanna's door open. She was gone. I ran outside and they were ridin' away. Susanna was wrapped up in a blanket. And Oscar was leadin' her horse. They had a pack mule and everything.'

Chance was numb. 'What did you do?'

'I ran in and got dressed. I went out to the corral and saddled my pony. But I couldn't keep up, and I lost them. They were heading due west, though.'

'How could you be sure?' Bragg asked.

'The stars. Our pa taught us how.'

'Then what?' Chance prodded.

'I didn't want Mr. Rawlins to find me, so I rode into the trees and circled the ranch, then I came back here, hoping to find you, Chance.'

'Bragg, you take Becky to the doctor's, where Patience can look after her.'

'What are you goin' to do?' Bragg asked.

'I'm goin' after Oscar. And that's a fact. You tell Drake if he comes to.'

'What about some sleep?'

'I'll sleep in the saddle.'

Becky stood up and threw her arms around Chance's neck, hugging him tearfully. She felt so tiny and helpless in his arms, a big lump came to his throat. Then she drew back, still anxious.

'Find her, Chance. She's scared of him.'

He nodded. 'Say a prayer, Becky.'

Bragg took the girl's hand and led her outside. The barkeep came forward, shaking his head.

'Listen, Darringer, you hang on a minute. I'll go back in the kitchen and load you up with some grub and supplies and a couple of canteens of water. Need a slicker?'

'I got one behind the saddle.'

'Let me throw in some cartridges. Save you time.'

It wasn't long before the barkeep came out with two sacks, a pair of canteens, and two boxes of cartridges. They shook hands and Chance hobbled into the dark street. He could see Becky and Bragg entering the doctor's house.

He knew Patience would take good care of her.

He tied the sacks behind his saddle, shoved the cartridges in his saddlebags, and mounted his stallion. He would have to get his bearings with the stars, same as Becky. But he traveled a lot by instinct. As he rode north up the street, he saw Patience run out of the house.

'Chance Darringer, you wait up!' she called. Chance reined to a halt, and she caught the bridle. 'You need a good tracker like me.'

'If I do, I'll come back. I'm a fair tracker myself. And no horse can keep up with this buckskin.'

'Maybe you're right. But you take my mare anyhow. You may need a spare. That country can get rough, especially if he turns into the mountains or heads north to the desert.'

She brought the gray mare over and handed him the reins.

Chance nodded his thanks. He watched as she transferred some of the supplies to the mare's saddlebags. Then she stepped back, saluting him. He nodded and smiled.

'Take care of Becky,' he said.

It was then that they saw the black dog trotting into town. It was panting and weary. It came up to Chance's mount and lay down, tongue hanging, yellow eyes fixed on Chance. It had broken away from Crandall.

Patience pointed. 'Now you have a real tracker.'

'All right,' Chance said. 'Hand him up, if you can.'

The animal didn't resist as she lifted it in the air. Chance caught it by the neck and foreleg, pulling it up and in front of him on the saddle. It settled against him, legs dangling, satisfied.

Chance set out, the moonlight spread before him. The mare kept easy pace with his stallion. He was in no hurry to wear down his mounts. This could be a long trail.

He was determined to find Susanna, and prayed she was all right. Saving her might help him feel less pain. He had been blaming himself for not helping Polly when he was needed. Now he had a chance to ease that misery by saving Susanna.

He'd bring Oscar back to face charges for trying to kill Drake. And somehow, he had to learn if Lynch or Oscar had killed Polly in Tombstone. But most of all, he had to try to save Susanna, even if he was riding into a bullet.

He slept in the saddle most of the way. The dog jumped down after a time and chose to walk on the ground ahead of him.

It was late morning when Chance arrived at the wooden gate in the barbed-wire fence. He rode through and onto the Rawlins's property. The sky was overcast and dark. He drew his leather coat more closely about him and pulled his hat down tight. It was plenty cold. He prayed it wouldn't snow.

Maybe it didn't make sense to take

time at the ranch, but he hoped that someone could give him a clue as to where Oscar might head.

When he arrived, all the hands were gone — or what was left of them. Tolliver, all crippled up from the cold, was the only one around. He came out of the bunkhouse, his white beard twitching. The dog licked his hand.

'Good to see you,' he greeted Chance.

Chance cut right to the point. 'You know where Oscar took Susanna?'

'Silas came out this mornin' and told the hands that they went off to Santa Fe to get married and wouldn't be back for a couple of months. He was annoyed because of the roundup comin' and the brandin' and markin' to be done.'

'And the little girl?'

'He set most of the men out lookin' for her. They found her tracks circlin' the ranch, then lost 'em. Some men are still lookin'.'

'Well, she's safe. And it seems like

Oscar ran off in the night, taking Susanna with him at gunpoint. They headed due west. He also tried to kill Marshal Drake.'

Tolliver's face tightened in anger. 'You're trackin' 'em?'

'Goin' to try.'

'I can't even get in the saddle, else I'd go with you. So'd Grimey, but he's out lookin' for the girl.'

'I'll go faster alone. You got any idea where Oscar is headin'?'

'No, but there's an old line shack that way. You'll get there by mornin'. And farther on, there's an abandoned homestead that's another day's ride. Here, I'll make a map.'

Tolliver scratched the dirt with his boot and explained what he was marking.

'Thanks,' Chance said. 'Now I want a word with Silas.'

'I wouldn't recommend it. He was hot as fire this mornin' when he found Oscar had taken off. You could see his tongue burnin'.'

'He may know something. Is he over at the house?'

Tolliver nodded. Chance rode over at the ranch house. He dismounted painfully and walked up to the door, ordering the dog to stay on the porch. Instead of knocking, he hobbled right inside.

Silas sat in his leather chair by the hearth. He nearly bit off his pipe when he saw Chance. His white hair and mustache looked unkempt. His eyes narrowed to slits as he stood up.

'What do you want, Darringer?'

'Susanna.'

'You're loco.'

'Oscar took her away at gunpoint. After he tried to kill Marshal Drake in front of witnesses.'

'What are you talking about?'

'That murder down in Tombstone. Marshal Drake found out that before she died, Polly stabbed her assailant with a pair of scissors, possibly on the back. Now, she was right-handed, so there could be a scar near the killer's back left shoulder. Your son got a mark like that?'

'My son never killed no woman.'

'When Drake tried to get Oscar to take off his shirt, your son beat him on the head with his rifle. Drake's near death right now. If he dies, your son will hang.'

Silas drew a deep breath. 'You're lyin'.'

'Your son is crazy, Silas. You must have known.'

Staggering to his feet, the old man picked up a paper from the table and shoved it at Chance. It was a handwritten note from Oscar saying they had gone to Santa Fe to get married and would be back in a few months. It added that he had taken the lawyer's papers for safekeeping.

'What lawyer's papers?' Chance demanded.

Silas sighed. 'You'll find out someday anyhow. Susanna's uncle, who died back East a long time ago, left a trust fund for Susanna when she turns twenty-one in July.'

'How'd you know that?'

'Her pa asked for help in contactin' the lawyer. Listen, you seen that little girl?'

'She's in town with Patience Smith.'

Silas shrugged. 'I'm glad for that.'

'I'm headin' after Oscar and Susanna.'

'All the way to Santa Fe?'

'No, they headed due west.'

Silas looked fatigued. He sank back in his chair, his head in his hands. Chance stood a moment, watching the hunched shoulders. This was a man who had wanted the whole valley, and for what? A son who had run away?

'While you're thinkin' things over,' Chance said, 'maybe you'd take that price off my head.'

Silas didn't look up. His shoulders were trembling.

Chance turned and walked toward the door.

He went outside into the cold and mounted his buckskin. With the mare trailing and the dog trotting ahead, he rode back to the bunkhouse, where Tolliver waited.

'Chance, you be careful,' Tolliver said. 'The old man's digesting what you told 'im, but pretty soon he's gonna start thinkin' he don't want his son arrested no matter what he's done. Silas is liable to set his gun hands on you. And you gotta come back this way.'

Chance thanked the man for his advice, and set out again. He headed due west, Tolliver's map in his mind. The dog kept ahead as if it knew where it was going. The weather was getting icy cold, and a brutal wind rose from the north. Snow would hide the trail.

He pushed his buckskin harder. As they climbed from the valley in the late afternoon, he saw clearer signs of the travelers. Rocks were rolled out of their sockets in the earth. Tiny bits of brush had been broken off. Dirt had been shifted. Hoofprints appeared now and then.

Two horses were making their way at

good speed with a pack mule trailing. The dog picked up the scent. Maybe he smelled Susanna.

Night fell, the sky heavy with clouds. There was no moon. Even though the dog had the scent, Chance was afraid of losing visible signs. He was forced to camp by a little creek in a hollow. Remembering Polly's death with agony and not wanting to find Susanna that way, he sat glaring at the flickering fire. The dog lay at his side.

★ ★ ★

While Chance worried through the night, a fire burned in a small iron stove in the abandoned line shack. A lamp cast an eerie glow in the single room.

Oscar chewed on some jerky and downed coffee. He sat on one of the bunks. Susanna was on the other, her white hands holding a cup of coffee. She was wearing her riding outfit, having been allowed to change from her night clothes the day before.

'You won't be sorry,' Oscar said. 'We'll be married in Prescott, unless there's a preacher at Camp Verde. I'll be a good husband, Susanna. We'll head for California, and make a new life.'

'But why? You had your father's ranch. I don't understand, Oscar.'

'You will someday.'

'I'm worried about Becky.'

'Don't be. Pa took a likin' to her.'

'Please, Oscar, let's go back.'

'Don't give me any trouble, Susanna.'

'But she's my sister.'

'Ain't her you're thinkin' of. It's that blamed Darringer.'

'No, Oscar. I'm promised to you.'

As he had the night before, he forcibly tied her hands behind her back with his lariat. If she struggled, he would slap her hard. Her face was bruised. He was too strong for her, and she didn't want to aggravate him until she found a way to escape.

Oscar took the end of the rope over

to his bunk and lay down, tying it around his waist.

'Please, Oscar, I can't sleep this way.'

He ignored her, and soon he was snoring. She lay on her side, her wrists already raw from the rope. Staring at him, her mind churning, she tried to make plans. She would need her horse and supplies to get back alive.

She felt released from her promise to her dying mother. Oscar was acting strange. He had taken her away at gunpoint, threatening to harm Becky if she didn't keep silent and do as he ordered.

There was madness in his eyes. She was frightened of what he might do. She would have to be careful and wait her chance.

Before dawn, they were on their way again. The sky was dark, and snow drifted down in silent, tiny fluffs of ice. It was beautiful in the foothills. Pines and aspens were scattered along the edges of the meadows.

★ ★ ★

A day behind them, Chance was trying to make up time. He came to the old line shack and saw where they had stayed. The dog now had the scent of Susanna for certain, and was excited.

They moved on, his stallion never seeming to tire. To his surprise, the mare kept pace. The dog trotted ahead, sniffing and waiting for them. When the light snow became too cold, Chance put the dog on the saddle in front of him and bent over the animal to protect it.

They came to the fence line. Barbed-wire lay in the wet grass. Oscar had cut it to cross quickly. But as Chance started to follow, he felt the dog spin and growl. The animal jumped down to the ground.

Turning in the saddle, Chance saw a rider coming along the fence. He stiffened, his gut tight. It was Lynch, his one good eye squinting in the brightness of the light snow. He wore a leather coat and rode a bay gelding. His rifle lay across the pommel.

As Lynch came up within ten feet of him, Chance readied himself for anything. But Lynch didn't have a gunfight in mind. He hadn't forgotten his beating back at the river.

'I knew you'd come this way, Darringer. Figured you could track Oscar, all right. But I been watchin' for you. I figure we got unfinished business. You're worth a heap of money besides. I could do a lot with five hundred dollars.'

'I'm in a hurry, Lynch.'

'It won't take long.'

'Maybe when I come back.'

Chance started to ride through the opening in the fence. The dog trotted on ahead. But Lynch snarled and dug his heels in, sending his bay charging like a locomotive into Chance's buckskin. Both horses reared and snorted.

At the same time, Lynch swung his rifle and hit Chance's shoulder. Angry,

Chance reached out and grabbed the barrel, jerking Lynch forward. Lynch grabbed his arm.

They struggled, then were thrown in midair by their horses. Struggling for the rifle, they crashed to the ground and rolled in the thin snow. Chance shoved his right fist in the man's mouth. Lynch clawed at Chance's face.

They rolled apart and sprang to their feet, breathing hard, sweat on their faces. Lynch pulled a knife, the long blade extended in the falling snow. Chance tried to concentrate, his leg throbbing with pain.

'This is it, Darringer. I'm gonna cut you up good and leave half of you out here for the vultures.'

Chance moved around him in a circle, watching as the knife slashed at him. Lynch was confident. He sneered as he cut the air.

'If you're scared, you can draw one of them fancy guns.'

Chance kicked hard with his good leg, hitting Lynch's hand. The knife flew in the air. Lynch tried to grab it and caught the blade. It cut his fingers and he yelped. At the same time, Chance dived in and pounded his face with a left and right, then a left. He hit the man's belly and shoved him backward.

Lynch staggered and fell on his back. Chance dropped on him, a knee on each side of his chest holding down his arms. The man gasped for air and struggled. His one good eye was wild.

Chance drew his right six-gun and shoved the barrel at the man's cheek as he held his head with his left hand. Lynch looked like he knew he was going to die.

'All right, Lynch. This is it. And that's a fact, unless you tell me who killed that girl in Tombstone.'

Lynch fought the barrel. 'Weren't me.'

'Tell me, blast it!'

'All right, sure.' Lynch choked on his fear but managed to talk. 'I was on guard. Oscar came ridin' back about an hour before sunup. He was hurt bad. He had a cut on his back, right below his left shoulder blade, like a knife got him. I helped him fix it. And he paid me to keep my mouth shut. He even paid me to kill you back at the river. And he's still payin'.'

'All right. We're goin' back to the line shack. And you're gonna peel your shirt, just to make sure.'

He hauled the battered man to his feet.

Back at the line shack, at gunpoint, Lynch peeled off his shirt. There were no knifelike scars on his back or chest. Chance left him on the floor, his hands tied behind his back and bound to his ankles. He left a fire burning and food where the man could eat it without his hands, and a canteen on the chair that could be tipped for water.

All the while, Chance had sensed that Oscar was his man.

Back on the trail, bent over in a slicker, he headed west again. But he was worried that the snow would hide the trail and kill the scent.

He was grateful for one thing. His leg was no longer throbbing or painful. It was just sore to the touch.

At the abandoned homestead the next day, he saw signs that Oscar and Susanna had been there. He moved on. The snow was still light, melting as soon as it landed on the ground. He prayed it would not get any worse.

He felt he was gaining time. That night, he talked to the dog at his side while a campfire warmed them under a rock overhang. Two feet farther from the fire, it was freezing.

'It ain't right, Pardner,' he said. 'She's too good for the likes of him. If he lays a hand on her, I'll kill him.'

The animal, crowded against him, looked up.

'I see now that Oscar's after her fortune, whatever it is. And she didn't know nothin' about it. And that's the wrong of it.'

The dog nestled its head on Chance's good thigh. He stroked the thick neck, his mind in turmoil.

'When she finds out she got all that money, she'll be headin' East, Pardner. She won't want to stay hereabouts. She'll want Becky to have a better life.'

Chance didn't sleep well that night.

In the morning, he was grateful that the sky was clearing. The snow had stopped, and none remained on the ground. The cold wind rose, cutting right through his leather coat.

He knew he was gaining because the dog was getting more excited. When he camped that night, he thought he could see the tiny glow of their campfire in the rise of the mountains far ahead. He resisted trying to traverse the treacherous rocks in the darkness. There was no moon.

* * *

At the distant campfire, Oscar was already checking his rifle. Susanna was distraught.

'How do you know it's Chance?' she asked.

'I could see him crossin' that meadow before dark, all right. It's not easy to miss that buckskin. I knew he'd be comin', and I'll be waitin'. But not here — I know a place where I can get him cold.'

'I won't let you do it.'

'If I don't kill that man, he'll take me back to be hanged. So you just shut your mouth.'

Susanna didn't understand fully, but she couldn't sleep that night, and not just because her hands and feet were tied.

In the morning, they rode up toward a rock canyon. The cliffs were red and spotted with snow. Only scrub junipers and chokecherries lined their path. A tiny creek ran down the canyon.

Oscar led the way through the canyon and tethered the horses in the clearing beyond. Susanna fought with him as he tried to tie her again. He slapped her so hard, she slumped unconscious to the ground. Then he bound and gagged her, tying her feet to the trunk of a small aspen. In a moment of kindness, he draped a blanket around her.

Then, rifle in hand, he began to climb up the rocks.

He knew he would soon have a safe perch and a good view of the head of the canyon. He would lie in wait.

He was going to kill Chance Darringer.

8

When Chance saw the narrow canyon ahead, he felt cold ripples up his back. The walls were about one hundred feet high, made up of rocks stacked on rocks. The dog didn't seem to hesitate as they headed for it. Still, the wind was at their backs.

Chance pulled out his Winchester and jerked the lever, sending a shell into the chamber. He felt shivers running up and down his spine. Sweat came to his brow.

As he neared, he saw the sunlight glance on a rifle barrel high on the left wall. He reined his buckskin about, but it was too late. A shot rang out.

The bullet creased the side of his head. Stunned, he fell from the saddle. The dog went charging up the cliff wall. Chance rolled onto the grass, unconscious.

Oscar grinned to himself and stood up, rifle in hand. He looked down at the rushing animal as it fought its way up, rock by rock. He picked up a huge stone and just dropped it down on the frantic animal's head. The dog went rolling down the wall and fell silent in the grass.

Oscar then started down slowly, taking his time, the wind blowing in his face. He was thinking of Prescott and California. Susanna in front of the preacher. Her fortune.

He reached the canyon floor, passed the body of the dog, and headed for Chance, who lay on his back in the grass. Oscar walked over to him and stood looking down at the lifeless man with blood on his temple. Chance lay with his eyes closed and mouth open. He looked dead for sure.

Oscar was pleased with his aim.

'Good-bye, Darringer,' he said, almost merrily.

Convinced that Chance was dead, Oscar took the reins of the buckskin and mare. He would leave Chance and his dog for the vultures. That made him smile.

He paused to kick the figure on the ground. Chance just lay prone, with no color in his face. Oscar thought of putting another bullet in him for satisfaction, but turned to look down the trail. There was no telling who else might be following.

After a long, pleasurable look at the body, Oscar led the horses up the canyon. When he reached the clearing, he saw that Susanna was awake and fighting her bonds. The gag was still in her mouth.

'Relax, honey, Darringer's dead.'

Her eyes widened. She stared at Chance's stallion. Then she closed her eyes tight as the tears came rushing forth. Oscar grunted and pulled the gag from her mouth.

'Go ahead and cry. You ain't gonna see him no more.'

She sobbed, choking on her tears. He untied her slowly.

'We gotta move on, honey. Just in case someone else followed.'

The will gone out of her, Susanna allowed him to jerk her to her feet. She wept and sobbed in the saddle. Her pain was unbearable, leaving her shattered and forsaken. Oscar was annoyed, but he figured she would come around in time. Either that or he would beat her into submission.

★ ★ ★

Back at the canyon entrance, lying on his back, Chance opened his eyes. Everything was blurry for a long moment. He was terrified he was blind. Then he saw the gray clouds above, moving gently in the sky. He heard a woodpecker in a distant tree, pounding at the bark.

And something was licking his face. It was the dog.

He sat up slowly, his head racked with pain and his body stiff from the cold. His rifle still lay in the grass some ten feet away where he had fallen. He still wore his six-guns. It must have pleased Oscar to leave him that way for others to find. It would show that Oscar had been brave against an armed Darringer.

He paused to shake the shock from his head. Then he stood up carefully. Recovering the rifle, he checked the chamber. It was ready to fire. Now if only he could find Oscar and Susanna. Furious that he had let himself be ambushed, he staggered over toward the canyon entrance. The dog trotted at his side.

As he walked to the clearing, he sensed that Oscar was long gone. He saw signs around a tree where Susanna must have been tied.

'Well, Pardner, we got a long walk ahead.'

Following the tracks of four horses and a mule was easy in the red dirt and spotted snow. Yet he knew he would have trouble catching them. As night fell, he was still far behind. They would stop, but he would not.

Weary, hurting, dazed, he continued on his way. But he was a Darringer, and he couldn't give up, no matter what happened. He staggered on in the darkness. At least they were on level ground, moving through pines and scant grass.

In time, he saw their campfire. It was a tiny glow in the distance. He sat down to rest. The dog snuggled close, and he stroked the big neck.

* * *

In the distance, Susanna huddled by the fire, eating beans from a plate while Oscar talked.

'We'll have a grand palace, honey, with some of that newfangled electricity. It'll be up high, where no one can look down on us. And fancy carriages. And we'll go to the opera. Would you like that?'

She listened but didn't answer. Maybe he had enough money in his saddlebags for that dream. She doubted it.

This time, she was too weary to resist as he tied her up with her hands behind her back and her feet fastened to the nearest tree. He covered her with blankets and bent down to kiss her.

'You'll see, honey. Everything will be fine.'

She had run out of tears. Dry-eyed, she watched him roll into his blankets. Then she whispered a prayer for deliverance. Her sleep was restless, and she dreamed of Chance.

In the morning, stiff from the cold, she sat up painfully. Oscar awoke at the same time. He stretched, pounded his chest a little, and smoothed his red beard. Then he came over to untie her. She was grateful. Maybe that was how he would beat her down, she thought. With kindness. Drawing her blankets around her, she moved to the fire.

They ate while he chattered about his big plans. Then he set about saddling her mare and his gelding. He talked about selling the stallion for a lot of money. Susanna listened in silence.

He kicked dirt over the fire and reached down to take her arm. As he pulled her to her feet, he suddenly froze.

Susanna followed his gaze. Ten feet from the fire stood Chance Darringer. She gasped in fright, but he wasn't a ghost. He was alive — a wonderful, joyous sight. Breathless, she lifted a hand toward him. Her heart was singing.

Oscar pulled her in front of him as he drew his six-gun. He pointed it to her ear. He snarled and laughed at the same time. His free hand was at her throat, choking her.

'So you weren't dead. Well, we can fix that.'

'Let her go.'

'Throw down that rifle. Drop your gun belt.'

Susanna desperately tried to free herself and couldn't. His grip was like a vise around her neck, cutting off her wind. She was losing consciousness, everything spinning before her.

'Drop it,' Oscar snarled.

At that moment, a blur of silent black fury sprang from the trees. The dog leaped on Oscar from behind and knocked him sideways. Susanna came free and fell to the grass, her hand to her throat as she gasped for air.

Oscar threw the dog off and hit it on the head with his pistol. Before he could turn and fire, Chance grabbed him by the arm and belt, jerked him to his feet, and knocked the gun from his hand.

Oscar grabbed him frantically. They struggled and fell to the ground. Oscar broke free and got up, kicking him. Chance caught the man's leg and twisted it. He reached up as Oscar fell toward him, grabbing his belt and throwing him over his head.

Oscar landed sprawled in the grass and rolled over. Chance got to his feet and rushed him, grabbing him by the neck and arm and throwing him again. Oscar pulled his knife, and Chance charged, struggling to take the weapon away.

Oscar fought like an animal, panting and gasping. He clawed at Chance's eyes and face. There was fury in his eyes as he shoved his knee in Chance's middle.

Still dazed from the wound on his head, weakened by the blows and his sore leg, Chance faltered. Yet he kept slamming his free fist in the man's face while the other hand fought for the knife.

They were on their feet, swaying wildly. The blade went flying in the air. Then Chance broke free and landed a series of deadly blows on the man's face and middle. Then he paused, for Oscar had dropped to his knees.

Chance drew his right six-gun and stood fighting for air as he spoke.

'Get up.'

Oscar took a while before he staggered to his feet. He was dizzy, battered, and exhausted. He glared at Chance.

'You ain't takin' me nowhere, Darringer. You'll be dead before they ever hang me.' Then Oscar looked past him at an approaching rider. 'See? There's my pa, comin' to save me.'

Chance blinked, trying to focus on the rider. To his surprise and delight, it was Drake. The lawman had a bandage around his head, yet he sat tall in the saddle.

Oscar's face turned to stone. He knew it was over.

Drake rode up and dismounted, six-gun in hand.

'I'll take over from here, Chance.'

Chance holstered his six-gun, his heart still pounding.

Oscar stared at Drake. 'So you ain't dead. And I ain't gonna hang.'

'Listen, Chance,' the lawman said. 'I saw where you had Lynch stashed at the line shack. He told me what he told you, that Oscar had come to camp with blood on him that last night in Tombstone. Oscar paid him to keep his mouth shut.'

'That's a lie!' Oscar said frantically.

'Let's have a look,' Chance said. 'Turn around.'

Oscar wouldn't move, so Chance reached over, grabbed Oscar's shirt, and ripped it open. A fat envelope fell on the grass as Oscar's chest was bared in the sunlight. Chance spun him around and saw two scars about an inch long just below his left shoulder blade.

Fury welled up in him. He grabbed the man by the neck with one hand and began pounding his face with the other. He heard his own voice roaring like some mountain cat.

It took all Drake's strength to haul him off the man. Oscar coughed and crawled on the ground.

'He killed Polly,' Chance sobbed, tears in his eyes.

'It was an accident,' Oscar yelled. 'I didn't mean nothin'! I was waitin' around town and saw her at the store. And I went to see her. But I was just tryin' to get her to be nice to me, that's all. I even tried to give her some money.'

Chance started to attack him again. Drake caught his arm and spun him back. Chance was so tired, his anger was melting away. Then he realized that nothing could bring Polly back.

Hot tears on his face, Chance picked up the envelope and turned to look at Susanna where she sat on the grass, the dog at her side. He walked toward her in a daze, feeling sick inside.

Tears trickled down Susanna's badly bruised face. She trembled all over. Handing her the envelope, he took her free hand and pulled her to her feet. He had to steady her so she wouldn't fall. She fell in his arms and hugged him. He hugged her back. His tears flowed in her soft hair. Her voice was a murmur in his ear.

'Is Becky all right?'

'Yes, she's with a woman in town.'

'I'm so glad you're here.'

Neither wanted to let go. He didn't care if Drake and Oscar were watching.

He was in pain, and Susanna felt like salvation. He found himself kissing the tears on her face. She reached up to wipe the moisture from his cheeks. He drew back and looked at her bruises. Even her throat was blue. He was glad she was alive. He turned from her slowly, releasing her reluctantly.

'You gotta ride past my pa, Marshal. And you ain't gonna make it,' Oscar snarled as Drake handcuffed him.

All the way back, Oscar kept promising they would never make it past the Rocking R. There was no way around it. Drake was nonplussed, as he planned to take Oscar down the river pass and unload him at Tucson. When they picked up Lynch at the line shack, Oscar fell silent and spent his time looking fiercely at the other man, who responded with an even meaner glare.

Their nights at the campfire were difficult, since Oscar tried to cause trouble. Lynch was always silent. But whenever the other men were asleep, Chance would look at Susanna, sitting in the firelight. It made him think of Polly over and over until he was sick again.

He felt numb. Susanna consoled him as best she could. She told him how her father had borrowed on her inheritance, leaving her with only five hundred dollars. She had given the papers to the marshal for safekeeping on the trail.

The morning they neared the Rocking R, it was obvious they had been seen. Ten gunmen, with Silas Rawlins in the middle, were waiting.

Oscar was delighted as they reined up in front of the men, who sat with rifles aimed at them. 'Pa, am I glad to see you. Get this marshal off my back.'

Drake was solemn. 'Your son beat a woman to death in Tombstone. There are two scars on his back where she stabbed him with her scissors. And he tried to kill me and my deputy here.'

'Pa, you gotta stop him.'

'There are too many witnesses,

Rawlins,' Chance said. 'And that's a fact.'

'Don't listen to him, Pa. We'll bury 'em. No one will ever know.'

'What about Susanna?' Chance asked.

'She'll be my wife. She can't say nothin'.'

Silas looked from one to the other. He'd have to kill Drake. And Chance. And maybe Susanna. Susanna was Becky's sister. How could he explain that to a little girl? Yet this was his only son.

Chance waved Susanna aside. She anxiously reined her mount out of the line of fire. Fear whitened her face so that the bruises looked drawn with blue crayon. She was in a panic and could do nothing. Chance wrapped the reins around the horn, freeing both hands.

Still, Silas hesitated. Oscar grew angry.

'Pa, you start shootin' or I'll tell 'em how you sent our men to burn out them ranchers. And you put that price on Darringer. That's against the law and you know it.'

Silas was in a tight spot, faced with his son's demands. Still, he knew he couldn't let Oscar hang. Not for anything, not even for a woman in Tombstone, or his own hide. But he couldn't raise his rifle. He couldn't start the carnage.

'Stand aside,' Drake ordered.

Suddenly, the man next to Silas pulled the trigger on his rifle. The shot creased Drake's arm. Everyone pulled and fired. Chance had two guns in his hands, firing rapidly. Bullets flew. Oscar ducked, hollering and trying to get his horse to move aside.

Four men died instantly. Silas was hit in the shoulder. Drake was hit on the arm and side, but he kept firing. A bullet grazed Chance's head near his old wound.

Silas tried to stop the bloodshed, but couldn't. It ended only when his last man fell from the saddle.

Silas straightened, blood on his shoulder. He looked around him at the dead men on the ground, the riderless horses. It was over with a shattering silence that lasted several minutes.

Oscar, unhurt, was stunned. 'Pa, help me!'

Unmoved, Silas turned away in silence.

Chance saw Grimey and Tolliver riding up from the ranch. He looked from Silas to the empty saddles. He hadn't wanted this. He was sick of death and wanted no more blood on his hands. Polly was avenged, and he was yearning to find a hole to hide in and spend his grief.

He turned to look at Susanna, who sat unharmed on her mount. She was pale and in shock, gripping the pommel with white fingers.

At the ranch, she tended their wounds before they continued to town. Silas would have allowed her to bandage him as well, but Maria insisted on caring for him herself. Silas stared up at her serene face as if he had never seen her before.

Susanna's hands trembled, yet Chance couldn't help but admire her determination to cleanse their wounds and bandage them. Afterward, she took time to pack a carpetbag for herself and Becky. They set out then, with Oscar and Lynch in tow. Silas didn't try to stop them from taking his son.

When the travelers reached town, it was late at night. Drake locked Oscar and Lynch in Bragg's storeroom and chained them to iron rings on separate walls. Then he and Chance went to the doctor, with Susanna trailing. Becky was ecstatic and rushed into Susanna's arms. Upon seeing the reunion, Patience offered to let Susanna and Becky stay with her.

Chance had his head checked and rewrapped. The doctor insisted they sleep in his spare rooms, since he had no patients.

But Chance walked outside into the darkness, seeking the cold air, trying to clear his head. Susanna followed.

'Chance, I'm so sorry about every-thing.'

He turned slowly and looked down at her in the starlight. Her voice was soft, her gaze anxious.

'What will you do now?' she asked.

'Go to Tucson with Drake, I guess. Be a witness.'

'Are you coming back?'

He shook his head. He was a walking misery. It could be years before he could bear the past. He was hurting so deep, he didn't believe he could recover. There was no room in his life for anyone, not anymore.

Sadly, Susanna turned and went back inside.

★ ★ ★

Four months later, after Bragg and Chance testified in Tucson, Oscar was sentenced to hang. Free to go, Chance said good-bye to Drake and thanked him. The next day he was on the trail to Tombstone. He visited Polly's grave and went to see her mother. He told the woman the killer was going to hang, and that he had loved Polly. She said Polly had had many suitors, but she had been waiting for Chance, having loved him at first sight. Somehow, the visit calmed him. He would always love Polly, but now he had found peace.

From then on, he began to think of Susanna. Her courage, that lovely smile, her sweet kiss, the way she had shared his pain. Her sadness when he left. She would have many suitors. As months passed, he became anxious. His life was unbearably empty and sad. He couldn't go on that way.

He wondered if it were possible for a man to be so lucky to love two women in a lifetime, and to be loved back.

And in the spring, worried he would be too late, Chance rode back into the valley. The aspens shone in the sunlight, and the green grass was still tall and plentiful. The familiar black dog trotted ahead of his buckskin.

At Antler, Bragg told him that Susanna and Becky were living with Patience. Susanna had many suitors, but she was still unattached. Patience and Crandall were getting married. Silas had sold the Rocking R and was gone, taking Maria with him. Bragg still had one thing in mind.

'You decided about being our sheriff?'

Chance shrugged. 'I'll let you know.'

He rode out through the valley. A lawman's job would enable him to earn some money. He was a good cattleman and knew horses. He would save and find a place of his own, build a spread, make a new life. But he didn't want to do it alone.

When he got to the apple orchard, he was impressed with Patience's irrigation ditches and fruit trees. He saw her riding toward him in a wagon behind a black horse. With her was Becky, wearing a dress with pink ribbons, and waving frantically. She ran over to pet the happy dog.

Patience smiled as he reined up

beside them. 'Chance Darringer. Well, I never.'

'I just heard you hooked old Maxie.'
She beamed. 'Wore him down.'

'Susanna's at the house,' Becky said.

'We'll make it a double weddin',' Patience suggested, slyly.

Chance grinned at her and tipped his hat. Then he waved them on and headed at a lope for the small, rambling farmhouse. He saw a garden and many colored flowers; fat white chickens were in the back pen. It looked like home. Now that he was here, he could hardly wait to see her. Loneliness surged through him.

He leaped down from his buckskin and charged up to the door, pushing it open and rushing inside. Standing by the table, momentarily frightened, was Susanna. The dog ran over to her. She reached down and patted its head. She stared at Chance in dismay.

She had been rolling dough and was covered with flour from head to toe. She had never looked more beautiful.

Wiping her face with the back of her hand, she came slowly around the table. Her blue eyes shone with tears. Chance was wild with joy.

'Susanna, will you marry me?' he blurted.

She didn't move. Her voice was hushed. 'Chance, there's something you have to know.'

His heart stopped in fear. Was there someone else? He was dazed by her hesitancy. He swallowed hard, trying to listen to her words, preparing for the worst. His pulse was wild. He had sweat on his face. He was in love with her and that truth was painful enough. To lose her now would be devastating.

'It's my inheritance, Chance. When you were here, I thought it was five hundred dollars. Then I finally read those papers. There were some zeros behind it.' She drew a deep breath. 'Every year, a very large bank draft will come in the mail.'

He felt as if a wall had sprung up

between them. He could fight a rival, but not this. He swallowed hard. 'So, what are you going to do?'

'I did just what I thought you'd do. I bought the Rocking R. Cattle and all. Grimey and Tolliver are running it. For us, Chance, and our children. And that's a fact.'

He was in a trance. Everything had gone crazy. She sensed his withdrawal. She took a step toward him, one floured hand held forth.

'Chance, I'd give it all away before I'd lose you.'

Stunned, he couldn't move. Then, slowly, he came to life. He had come too far to turn back now. He began to smile with joy as her words hit home. He grinned happily.

'No, don't do that.'

She brightened. 'It's all right, then?'

He held out his arms. She rushed forward, covering him with flour as she hugged him. He found her sweet, soft lips. She tasted delicious and smelled like apple pie. She would be his life, his home, the mother of his children. She felt wonderful.

She wiped the flour from his face and laughed.

He began kissing her again. This time, forever.

THE END

Lee Martin also writes under the pseudonym of Lee Samuels, M. Lemartine and Lee Phillips.

We do hope that you have enjoyed reading this large print book.

Did you know that all of our titles are available for purchase?

We publish a wide range of high quality large print books including:
**Romances, Mysteries, Classics
General Fiction
Non Fiction and Westerns**

Special interest titles available in large print are:
**The Little Oxford Dictionary
Music Book, Song Book
Hymn Book, Service Book**

Also available from us courtesy of Oxford University Press:
**Young Readers' Dictionary
(large print edition)
Young Readers' Thesaurus
(large print edition)**

For further information or a free brochure, please contact us at:
**Ulverscroft Large Print Books Ltd.,
The Green, Bradgate Road, Anstey,
Leicester, LE7 7FU, England.
Tel:** (00 44) **0116 236 4325
Fax:** (00 44) **0116 234 0205**

A LAND TO DIE FOR

Tyler Hatch

There were two big ranches in the valley: Box T and Flag. Ben Tanner's Box T was the larger and he ran things his way. Wes Flag seemed content to play second fiddle to Tanner — until he married Shirley. But the trouble hit the valley and soon everyone was involved. Now it was all down to Tanner's loyal ramrod, Jesse McCord. He had to face some tough decisions if he was to bring peace to the troubled range — and come out alive.

THE SAN PEDRO RING

Elliot Conway

US Marshal Luther Killeen is working undercover as a Texan pistolero in Tucson to find proof that the San Pedro Ring, an Arizona trading and freighting business concern, is supplying arms to the bronco Apache in the territory. But the fat is truly in the fire when his real identity is discovered. Clelland Singer, the ruthless boss of the Ring, hires a professional killer, part-Sioux Louis Merlain, to hunt down Luther. Now it is a case of kill or be killed.

GOING STRAIGHT IN FRISBEE

Marshall Grover

Max and Newt were small-time thieves, a couple of unknowns, until the crazy accident that won them a reputation and a chance to reform. But going straight in a town like Frisbee was not so easy. Two tough Texans were wise to them and, when gold was discovered in that region, Frisbee boomed and a rogue-pack moved in to prey on prospectors. In the cold light of dawn, the no-accounts marched forth to die.

W